"Ah," she said, looking at the picture. "It is David. I would have known him anywhere. And there is the scar! The same scar. It shows yet."

"Scar?" said Angela, leaning over to look closer. "I never noticed a scar before. What scar do you mean?"

"Why, the one he got when he saved you from the fire! How he ever got you down those stairs and out safely, nobody ever knew, but he accomplished it, at this price!" and she pointed to the scar.

Angela picked up the picture and studied it again. Yes, that was a scar! Why had she not known it before? And could it be that she had been the cause of it?

The Honeymoon House

GRACE LIVINGSTON HILL

LIVING BOOKS
Tyndale House Publishers, Inc.
Wheaton, Illinois

Living Books is a registered trademark of Tyndale
House Publishers, Inc.

"The Honeymoon House," "Life out of Death,"
"The Minister's Son," and "The Old Guard" were
originally published in 1938 by the J. B. Lippincott
Company.

Fourth printing, Living Books edition, December 1988

Library of Congress Catalog Card Number 87-50132
ISBN 0-8423-1366-4
Copyright 1984 by Robert L. Munce Publishing Co.
All rights reserved
Printed in the United States of America

CONTENTS

THE
HONEYMOON HOUSE

*I go to prepare a place for you ... I will come again
and receive you unto myself.* JOHN 14:2, 3.

ANGELA was lovely, there was no denying that. When she glanced up from her
drawing and her clear eyes looked
straight into yours from under those level
pleasant brows, you did not wonder at the gorgeous
diamond she wore upon the third finger of her left
hand. She seemed altogether lovely and greatly to be
desired.

She had delicate features and rich dark hair that
curled away from her white forehead entrancingly.
She had a ravishing smile and a look of character
about her whole sweet being. Those who watched
her daily admired and loved her greatly and felt that
the man whose promised wife she was had a rare
future before him.

She sat at her work in the bay window where a
glint of light touched the waves of her lovely hair,
and brought out the delicate coloring of her rounded

cheek and the clear light in her eyes. Her friend Ellen, entering, paused to take in the picture and put it away in her memory as a precious treasure.

"Good morning, Angela," she said as the girl looked up, her pencil poised for another skillful line in her drawing. "You're just a picture as you sit there. I wish I had my camera with me. I'd like to have that expression to keep. I'd like to make a copy and send it to David. I know he'd love it!"

Angela smiled indulgently. "You are a dear old flatterer," she said, "and David has already more pictures of me than he knows what to do with. It isn't really necessary for him to have another. Sit down, won't you? Excuse me for going right on working; I must finish this drawing and get it in the late morning mail. But I would love to have you stay and talk to me while I work."

"Well, then, tell me the news! When is David coming back?"

Angela smiled contentedly. "Oh, sometime, I suppose. He doesn't say just when."

"But aren't you awfully impatient to see him? I don't see how you can possibly stand this long separation. He was always so devoted."

Angela smiled. "I'm pretty busy, you know," she said, with a proud little lift of her head. "I'm getting ready to earn my living, and I'm doing quite well, they tell me. I've even got a few orders of my own. This is an order I'm working on now. Of course I haven't finished my apprenticeship yet in the office, but they are letting me do a few little things on the side for people who don't want to pay the head architect and the head decorator's prices. See what I'm doing. Isn't this going to be the prettiest room? It's a great ugly square room we're making over, in a country house. See this bay window! Isn't that delightful? And I'm putting a seat all around it upholstered in blue velour. There's a wonderful rug for the floor, the loveliest old Chinese blue, and the furniture is perfect; rare old specimens. I picked them up cheap here and there—at least, I got a price on them, and I think the owner will take them when he sees this picture. I'm so enthusiastic about my work, and it's such fun to earn my own money!"

"It's lovely," said the friend, looking over Angela's shoulder, "but—what will you do with it all when you are married?"

"Married?" Angela lifted sweet eyes vaguely. "Oh, that's a long time off yet! I haven't thought much about that. Of course that will come sometime, but just now my business is to succeed and begin earning my own living. I'm here, and David is away. My main thought has to be put on my work right here and now."

"But David was so impatient to be married."

"Well, he is, I guess," said Angela. "But we can't be married till he gets back, you know, and why should I just sit around and harp on that when I can't do a thing about it?"

"But isn't he succeeding in what he went to do?" asked the friend, puzzled.

"Oh, yes, I think he is. I haven't had time to write very long letters, and I haven't asked him much about it, but he seems satisfied with his work."

"But doesn't he say a word about when he will be done and be coming back?"

"Oh, yes, now and then. But he doesn't say when. Several times he has said he might surprise me someday. The last letter, I believe, said it might be soon!"

"Why, he might be coming today!" exclaimed the friend.

"Oh, I hardly think so!" Angela smiled contentedly.

"But I should think you'd be so thrilled about it you couldn't do a thing!" said the friend, looking at her calm face wonderingly.

"Why should I get thrilled about something that I don't know a thing about?" said the girl pleasantly. "Time enough to get thrilled when it happens—*if* it happens. You know, I never wanted him to go away at all. I wanted him to stay right here and get into business in this part of the world and begin to be a success. But no, he had to run away to the other side of the world, and I just couldn't understand it. So I got to work to improve myself, and improve the time while I was waiting."

"But aren't you writing all the time to beg him to come at once?"

"Why, no, it doesn't seem quite nice to talk about it."

"But I should think you just couldn't stand being separated so long. He's such a wonderful man!"

"Yes, he is rather wonderful, isn't he?" said Angela calmly. "But I'm not worrying. He's doing his work and I'm doing mine. I really couldn't spare much time to go about with him just now, if he *were* here. I want to succeed. In the end he'll come, of course, but I hope by that time to have reached my ambition. Do you know what I want to do? I want to build a house for us to live in! I want to build it all myself, and furnish it before he gets here, and I want to have reached the place where I am self-supporting!"

"Oh, but do you think he would like that?" asked her friend, astonished. "I think a man always wants to feel he can take care of his wife."

"Oh, that's the old-fashioned way of looking at things, of course, but I shouldn't like to have to depend on somebody else for everything. I'd rather earn my own money and my own position in life."

"But David would be grieved, I'm sure," said the friend. "I remember hearing him tell my mother how happy he was going to be, providing for you as a lady should be provided for. I remember his look when he said it; a kind of light seemed to glow all over his face as if it came from within. 'She shall have the best that is to be had!' he said with a great tenderness in his voice. 'It is going to be my delight to work for her and get her all that she wants.' "

"Oh, yes, he's very sweet," said Angela easily. "He writes that way sometimes, too. But I feel a girl is much more independent when she has an income and a business of her own. Her husband respects her more, and they get on better."

"But Angela, dear, not a *house!* You wouldn't try to build the house that you two are to live in! Build a house *for sale*, perhaps, but not the house you will go to as a bride. It would hurt him. I'm sure it would hurt him."

"Oh, no, not when he sees the house. It's going to be the darlingest little nest of a place, and yet spacious too, and with all the loveliest contrivances for comfort and beauty. You see, no man understands what kind of a house a girl wants, and if I get it all fixed up before he comes, why, he's sure to like it, and there won't be any difficulty about details."

"But, my dear, how do you know he will be willing to settle where you build your house?"

"That's just it. I want to make it impossible to go away from my business. I'm expecting to have established a big business by the time he comes, a business that will be really worthwhile. I don't intend to run any risks of having to leave it. If the business is here and the house is here all ready for a home, he couldn't help but like it."

"Oh, Angela dear, I'm afraid you are making trouble for yourself. No man likes his bride to get the home ready. That is *his* place."

"But David loves me, you know." Angela smiled with calm assurance, making a neat little picture of a chair with her sharp pencil point in the room she was building.

There was silence for a moment while her friend tried to think how to make it plain to her.

"But hasn't *he* said anything about the details of your home, where it shall be, and what kind of a house he means to prepare for you?"

"Oh, yes, I believe he has mentioned such things once or twice. But I usually save his letters to read at night just before I go to bed, and sometimes, to tell you the truth, I'm so worn out with the work of the day that I don't always read them through. I fall asleep."

"You don't read his letters through!" said Ellen aghast. "The letters of a lover like that?"

"Oh, I generally read most of them. When I have time I read them through. They really are lovely letters. His diction is exquisite sometimes. It reads just like poetry. But when one is hard at work on practical things it is often difficult to get into the clouds and read dreams of loveliness."

"Oh, Angela!" protested her friend. "You don't realize how wonderful it is to have a lover who takes time to write you long letters and tell you all his beautiful poetic dreams for you."

"Oh, I write to him every day myself, of course," said Angela a bit haughtily, as one would say, "I always say my prayers." "You know I am as busy as he is, and he ought to be glad I take time to write."

Angela's friend gave her a strange, half-pitying look.

"What do you write about?" she said softly.

"Oh, I write about my work. I tell him every little detail. I try to make him appreciate the color schemes I am working out in the rooms I decorate, and the symmetry of line in the buildings I draw. You see, I want him to understand and appreciate the loveliness of the house I have built, when I get it done. And so I keep him in touch with my own progress. I want him to know how well I am doing, so that he will appreciate me too, you know, and see how I am working to prepare this home in my native land."

Angela paused to make it plain on her drawing where the windows were located and which way the doors swung, before she went on again.

"Writing letters like that serves two purposes," she said. "It counts as a letter to David, and it serves to keep clear in my mind all that I have accomplished during the day. It is excellent discipline for the mind. And he cannot fail to see what a helper he is getting in marrying me, someday."

"But when is that day to be, dear?" asked her friend again. "Aren't you eager for its coming?"

"Oh, so-so!" said Angela with a ripple of laughter. "I'm having a grand time. I love my work and I want to get on. I'm earning real money and putting it where it will tell for the most! And evenings now and then I have a wonderful time with some of my friends."

"But don't you ever feel sad when you see the other girls with their fiancés, to think yours is so far away?"

"Oh, there are always plenty of men who are willing to show me a good time if I can spare an evening," said Angela carelessly. "I went out with Herbert Boone last night to a party. We had a wonderful evening with the old crowd, and stayed out so late that I'm really sleepy today in consequence."

"Herbert Boone? Why, Angela! I thought he was a bitter enemy of David. I thought he had once threatened David's life."

"Oh, well, one can't stop on little things like that.

Besides I only go with him occasionally."

"And does David know?"

"Why, really, I'm not sure whether I ever mentioned it to David or not."

"But, my dear, isn't that rather disloyal to David? His confessed enemy?"

"Oh, darling!" Angela laughed. "How old-fashioned you are! One doesn't stop to consider little differences between men friends when one goes out to have a good time of an evening! Really, darling, where have you been these last few years that you haven't seen that people have dropped that old code and choose their friends where they like? Why, Nan Lacey goes around quite a bit with the present wife of her former husband and nobody seems to mind."

"But a sworn enemy of your beloved, Angela, one who has tried to kill him on more than one occasion."

"I'm sure David wouldn't mind my doing it in the least," said Angela lightly. "He was always broad-minded. And really, we behave so well that I wouldn't mind taking even David himself along with us. Anyway," with a toss of her head, "he can't mind what he doesn't see."

"But won't he feel it, dear? Those things are subtle, and they hurt."

"Well, *he* went away, didn't he? He left me here alone, didn't he? He can't expect me to sit and mope forever, can he?"

"Ah, but he went away to get ready to be with you always. He went away to prepare for you to be with him."

"That's all right when the time comes," said Angela with a light laugh. "I'm not married yet."

"But doesn't he give you any intimation how soon to expect him? Haven't you any guide as to what to expect?"

"Oh, yes, he talks a lot about it, but in such a strange way," said Angela with a bit of a frown. "Sometimes I can't make out what it is all about. He mixes up sort of fairy stories, about flowers and trees and rain. Once when I asked him how soon he was coming he talked about the fig tree budding. He speaks about the summer rain, and a prince from the North, and education, and new inventions, and all sorts of queer things. I can make nothing of it. Such fanciful language. Not long ago he wrote, 'We shall feed among the lilies,' and goodness knows I don't want to go camping! I have given up trying to understand him. You know he has been away since before my father and mother died, and has been talking about coming back ever since. But he hasn't come yet. I don't think he means to come for a long, long time, and I'm just as well satisfied, for I want to get on in the world before he comes."

"And yet you are wearing his ring on your finger."

"Oh, yes, we are engaged!" said Angela with a bright smile.

"And you love him still, Angela?"

"Why, yes, of course I'm fond of him," said Angela a bit crossly.

"I wonder if you remember him well, dear?"

"Of course I do, and if I didn't he is always sending me pictures. I couldn't forget him."

"Pictures? You mean photographs?"

"Yes, photographs and snapshots. He seems to want me to keep in close touch with him, but he doesn't in the least realize how busy I am. Sometimes I don't have time to open the pictures for days. Now that I think of it, one came yesterday, and I haven't opened it yet. I just couldn't stop. This drawing has to be in the mail this morning."

"I'm hindering you!" said her friend self-reproachfully.

"Not a bit," said the girl, writing her name with a tiny flourish at the bottom of the drawing. "I'm all done now. I've only to put this in the mailing tube and address it, and then I'm at leisure for the rest of the day. I'm glad you came in."

"But aren't you going to open your picture, Angela? I'd like to see how David looks now. That is, if you don't mind my seeing it right off. Perhaps you want it all to yourself the first day or two, and if so I won't intrude."

"Oh, mercy no! I'm not sentimental like that. Here, I'll give you the package and you can open it while I address this."

"But you oughtn't to do that!" protested the friend. "Think how he would feel if he knew that you had let another open the package that he did up for your eye to see first."

"Nonsense! That's ridiculous. Open it, please! I may forget it for another week if you don't."

There was silence while Angela wrote, and the friend cut the string and unwrapped the picture.

"Ah!" she said, and was still again. "It is David! I would have known him anywhere. And yet, he seems older, somehow sadder!"

"Sad?" said Angela offendedly. "What has he to be sad about?"

She came and stood by her friend and looked at the picture over her shoulder.

"I wouldn't be expected to know," said the friend.

"Well, he certainly has everything his own way!" said Angela. "He went away in spite of all that I could do, and he seems to be staying as long as he pleases. I don't see why he should be sad."

"Is he sure of you, Angela?"

"Sure of *me?*" said Angela, now thoroughly annoyed. "What has that to do with being sad?"

"If you are his, and he isn't sure of your love, then there would be good reason."

"Goodness, how silly you are! Silly and sentimental! David and I fully understand each other, so you needn't get any such notions."

There was another long silence while the two looked at the picture.

"I don't like the way his hair is cut!" said Angela in a cross voice. "I'll have to write to him about that. It's most unbecoming. I like to have things beautiful. He used to be so handsome."

There was another silence, and then the friend spoke quietly, almost as if she were speaking to herself.

"And that is *the scar!*" she said sorrowfully. "The same scar. It shows yet!"

"Scar?" said Angela, leaning over to look closer. "I never noticed a scar in his pictures before. I guess he usually has the other side of his face taken. But what scar do you mean? He didn't have any scar that I saw when he went away."

"The scar he got when he saved you from the fire!"

"Did he get his face scarred then? I didn't know it! I was sick, you know, for a long time; and before I got up he went away. He only came at night to say good-bye. That was when he put this ring on my finger."

"Yes, he was scarred very badly on one side of his face. But the doctors grafted on skin. I understood it was healing, but it seems to show in the picture."

"Oh, I don't think that is a scar at all! It is just a blemish in the picture. I wouldn't like to think he got scarred saving me. I'm sure it was utterly unnecessary. He always did insist on doing unnecessary things for me, when I could perfectly well do them for myself. I'm sure I could have walked out of a burning building as well as he did, if he hadn't picked me up and made it impossible."

"My dear, you were unconscious! Yes, he found you lying in a room that was all aflame! You were as good as dead when he struggled away from the firemen who were trying to prevent his going back to find you. He went through smoke and flame, and found you lying unconscious on the floor. A moment after he started down the stairs with you in his arms the ceiling of that room fell! And the floor fell through to the next story below. How he ever got you down those stairs nobody ever knew, but he accomplished it, at this price!" and she pointed to the scar.

"Oh, I'm quite sure you are mistaken!" said Angela pertly. "Such things are always exaggerated afterward, and it's a long time ago. I suppose people have talked in town and made a lot of it."

"Didn't David ever tell you about it?"

"No, I never encouraged him to. I was too upset before he went away, and when he wrote and mentioned anything about the fire I just skipped that. I hate gruesome stories!"

"Oh, but Angela, he loved you! And he saved you! And he'll surely come back to you."

"Yes, I suppose so," said Angela, twisting her gorgeous ring about her finger, "but somehow I cannot make it seem real anymore."

"But suppose he should be coming tomorrow, or even tonight, dear?"

Angela laughed.

"He wouldn't come like that. He's been away a long time. He's not any more likely to come tomorrow than he was to come all of the yesterdays."

"But he might have come then. Were you ready to meet him?"

"Well, no, frankly, there's a lot I want to do before I leave home."

"But oughtn't you to get ready? If you're going to be with him the other things that you might do wouldn't matter, would they? If I were you I'd get everything ready."

"Ready?" Angela laughed. *"Ready!* According to

him I don't need to do a thing. What do you think
that absurd man wrote me a few days ago? He said I
wouldn't need to prepare a wedding dress. He said
he was going to *bring* me one when he came! *Imagine* it! Being married in a dress *a man* had selected!
I wrote and told him nothing doing! I told him I pre-
ferred to select my own wedding dress!"

"Oh, Angela! How could you! Don't you know
that's the old oriental custom for the bridegroom to
give the bride her outfit? He meant it for a delicate
attention. It has a wonderfully sweet meaning."

"Delicate attention indeed!" sneered Angela,
making her lips look as unpleasant as such beautiful
lips could look. "I'm not an oriental, and this is the
modern world. I prefer the customs of today!"

"Oh, but Angela, you don't understand him. You
are hurting him! My dear, I wish you would write
and tell him you are glad he has done such a lovely
thing. I know you will be glad you did it. I just feel it
is something lovely! I knew him years ago and he has
a very beautiful soul. You would be glad, I know, if
you did it."

Angela's eyes suddenly flashed fire and her
straight placid brows grew stormy.

"Really!" she said haughtily. "I do wish you would
mind your own business! I can't see why you think
you have any right to pry into mine, and then offer
suggestions! It is *I* who am engaged to David, not
you. And I shall conduct my own affairs as I see
best."

"I'm sorry," said the friend, rising and brushing
away the tears from her eyes. "I love you both and it

has been so wonderful to think of you loving each other. I can't bear to see such an ideal companionship hurt in any way. I only thought, what if he should come and you not be ready for him! It would be so dreadful for him to come and find you out enjoying yourself with his enemy."

Angela laughed.

"Spare yourself," she said disagreeably. "He has no idea of coming at present, I am sure, and by the time he does come I'll very likely have attained my ambition and be ready to see him. Anyhow, he'll have learned a lot, and not be so sentimental."

"Angela, excuse me, dear, I must just say this. You know it isn't exactly sentiment, what a man feels for the one whose life he has saved. I was looking at your beautiful face this afternoon and thinking how it was his doing that you were not all scarred and dreadful for life instead of himself. Your beautiful face might have been a dead face if he hadn't risked his own life and manly beauty to save yours. You owe him your life and beauty, Angela, and you mustn't hurt him. If he brings you a wedding dress you must wear it and be glad, whatever it is."

Angela laughed.

"Even if it should be only white linen?" she queried comically. "That's what he says it is!"

"Yes, even if it should be white linen," said her friend solemnly. "Listen, Angela dear, I can't get away from the thought of you lying white and still on the cot in the firehouse, and David lying grimed and swathed in bandages on the floor not far away. His hands and feet wrapped in bandages, his face covered with bandages. Oh, Angela! How he loves you! Old Tim Morgan, the fire chief, told me once that the minute he came out of his swoon he asked for you, and when they said you were coming around all right, and were not scarred at all, he said 'Thank God!' and swooned away again! Angela, he loves you with a love that is worth all other treasures of earth. Be good to him, Angela, be persuaded—"

"Oh, for heaven's sake!" said Angela, now thoroughly angry. "Am I a babe in arms to be dictated to about my love affairs? Kindly change the subject, won't you? Come, I've got to go out and mail this drawing. Will you come with me? And for pity's sake, forget David and let's talk about my business career."

"But if he should come for you soon, Angela?" ventured the friend again.

"Well, there's no chance of his coming for a long time, if he comes at all," said Angela. "Come! Now let's be a little cheerful."

But after she had parted from her friend and turned back toward her home, she could not get away from the words Ellen had spoken about David. Somehow a picture of him as she had known him at first came back to her mind—handsome, bright, the most admired boy among her schoolmates. How proud she had been to have him choose her to walk with, carrying her schoolbooks, accompanying her everywhere. How gorgeous her diamond had seemed when he first put it upon her finger, before worldly ambition had taken root in her heart.

The picture of him was so vivid as he used to be in their school days that when she reached her room she took out the picture again and sat looking at it.

Yes, those were the same eyes that looked out at her, only the sparkle had gone out of them. She could see what her friend had meant by saying he looked sad. What had made him this way? Had she had anything to do with it?

She recalled how empty her letters had been of late, mere descriptions of the rooms she was creating for the notable decorators and architects for whom she was working. She had written over and over again about her own success. And letter by letter his own had grown more grave and sad, except for that lily-language toward the end, that talk of "my beloved in the garden" that she had not understood. It was as if she were very far away from him, separated by a thick veil.

Yet it had been his own doing that he had gone away. She picked up the picture that had fallen in her lap and studied it again. Was that a scar or had it been the mere imagination of her friend?

Yes, that was a scar! There was no mistaking it! Why had she not known it before? Could it be that she *had* been the cause of that scar? She could not bear the thought. The tears were gathering in her eyes in spite of all her resolves. She brushed them away fiercely and looked harder at the picture, which seemed to look back at her, steadily, sorrowfully. Was it also accusingly? Oh, could that be true?

Presently she could bear it no longer, and flinging the picture into a drawer out of sight she put on her hat and went down to the firehouse seeking the fire chief. She must know the truth of this, once and for all. Did she owe her life to David? Or was this all a fantasy of her friend's imagination?

The fire chief was embarrassed when the beautiful girl came seeking him. He had long watched her from afar and curled his lip at her indifference, at the ingratitude of a girl whose life had been saved at such fearful cost to her lover; she seemed to have forgotten him. But now he dropped his eyes before her loveliness and knew not what to say.

At last her pleading unlocked his grim old lips and he told her the story in detail, not sparing her. He even took a kind of pleasure in seeing her lips quiver, and her body wince as the story went on. David was to him a very great hero, and he did not spare description when it came to his sufferings in this girl's behalf. He had visited him in the hospital. He had himself taken David, at his own insistence, to visit Angela that night before he left for a foreign land where he had business. He knew how unfit David had been to make that farewell call. He knew what it had cost him to go the jeweler's and select that diamond, what pain he endured when he came to say good-bye. And when Angela left the firehouse she knew all about it too.

She went back to her beautifully appointed suite of rooms where she worked, and took his picture out again. She took out all the pictures that he had sent her, to try and piece the story together. She studied the scar on his face which had suddenly grown wondrously dear, and she wept over it. Looking at his picture now, and knowing all that he had done for her, she began suddenly to see herself, as if a picture of her own petted life were there in the frame beside his. She saw the selfishness in her heart. She saw how she had treated him, and how she must have hurt him! Such love as his had been! She remembered how she had been dancing gaily through the days since he left, filled with her own ambitions, her own desire to reach the place in her chosen profession. She thought of her desire to design and execute the house of her dreams, and fill it with all the lovely things in which she delighted. She had scarcely had a thought of him from one week's end to another. Going out with other men, she had amused herself flirting with a world that was alien to all that he loved. Even seeking pleasure with his enemy!

All this she saw and bowed her head in shame and wept again. Ah! Such love! And such unforgivable scorn and indifference as she had given in return! He would not love her now if he knew what she really was, what she had become since he had gone away!

Then suddenly she was seized with a great desire to read his letters over again, every one from the beginning. It would be torture to her soul, but she would read them. And then, somehow she must muster courage to confess her past disloyalty and indifference! She must return his gorgeous ring, that she had so loved to flaunt in the eyes of her world, that they might the more admire and worship *her*. She saw now that she had used his love simply to further her own ends.

So she began to read, and her heart was more and

more humiliated till her tears flowed so that she could scarcely see the written words.

There were many paragraphs which had not meant a thing to her when she had first read them so hastily. But now, in the light of what she knew he had done for her, their meaning was suddenly revealed, and her heart was thrilled with his great love and tenderness.

And then she came to the most humiliating letters of all. Those she had not even opened. And lo, she found that he *knew all about her!* He had kept in touch with her movements from afar. He told her in those letters how he knew just what she had done; he knew all her selfishness and indifference and her disloyalty to him, and yet he said he loved her still! "With an *everlasting* love!" he said. He told her that he would forgive and *forget* what she had done! That he would put her disloyalty behind his back, he would drown her indifference in the depths of the sea, her selfishness and ambition and sin he would remember no more! He would put all those things "as far as the east is from the west." Because he had gone through death for her he would count these things as though she had never done them. Such love! It was unbelievable!

And she, what should she do? There was no longer need for her to confess her sins, for he already knew them. It only remained for her to acknowledge them.

But, yes, there was one more thing she could do! She could own to him that now she really loved him. Too late for her to win his admiration and respect, of course. Too late for him to see in her all that a bridegroom had a right to see in his bride. But even so, at last she had found out her mistake, and her punishment was that she loved him with a love that burned through her shamed and humiliated soul like a sword thrust. So far as she was concerned, she was *his,* and his *forever,* now, whether he wanted her or not.

But now as she looked at the dates of these long-ago letters, and remembered that she had never answered them except by long accounts of her own works and ambitions, and by worldly requests for him to do something more for her, she began to feel that surely, since that letter of forgiveness, he must have cast her off forever! He had written her full pardon weeks ago, and she had not even so much as referred to it. If he knew that she had not even taken the trouble to read it, surely he would feel that that was unforgivable!

She looked at that latest picture again and now she saw the scar standing out clearly. Had he sent that to remind her how he had suffered for her? Ah, could she ever by a life's devotion make him believe that now she really loved him, as a bride should love?

She remembered that before he went away he had said that he was going to prepare a place for her. Shame covered her anew when she thought of her own ambitions to build a house in her own land that should be strong and enduring, and with but grudging room for him, and no thought whatever of the place he had been preparing for her. Did he know that too?

But while she thought upon all this her telephone

began to ring. At first she ignored it, for she would not be interrupted in this searching of her soul. But finally its insistence annoyed her and she reached out and took down the receiver.

"This is Western Union," said a voice. "A telegram! Will you take it now?"

Angela's heart almost stopped beating. Had something happened to David? How terrible if she was never able to tell him of her shame and sorrow! How terrible if she could never tell him how she loved him now, how all was changed, and how repentant she was. If David should be dead! If she could never thank him for bearing the scars for her!

The operator's voice came insistently: "Will you take the message now?"

She heard her own faltering voice saying yes, and then the operator again:

"Have prepared a mansion. Am on my way to get you. Be watching! I shall be there soon. There may be some delay, yet I *may* be there today! I love you.
David."

Then Angela's heart leaped with joy! He knew it all, and yet he loved her! He was coming soon! He had prepared a mansion! And he would be bringing her wedding dress!

Suddenly she sprang up. He had told her to watch! He might be coming any minute now! And there was a great deal for her to do before he came. Could she accomplish it all?

She gave not a thought to her life ambition, her careful drawing from which she had hoped to win a prize that would set her feet on the high road to success. She had forgotten it entirely. She was going home with her bridegroom to the mansion he had prepared for her. There was much to do, but not anything of her own devising. There were things that he had asked her to do before he went away. She had forgotten all about them in her absorption in herself. He had given her messages that he had asked her to deliver to some of his friends, and to people in whom he was interested—messages of hope and cheer and help to people in sorrow and distress—and she had not even remembered them until now.

Also he had asked her to look up some of his relatives who were to be invited to the wedding and get to know them before the wedding day. He wanted her to love them as he did. Oh, there was a great deal to be done and so little time in which to do it! How could he ever forgive her for her negligence of those he loved? Her carelessness about giving the help he had sent? So much to be done, and *perhaps* only the rest of this day in which to do it!

She arose hastily and prepared to go out on his errands, but as she was just ready to go, a caller came to see her about some work he wanted done. He was one of the great men of the earth. He had seen her drawings and had chosen her to do a huge building planned for amusement and entertainment, an operation that would be known throughout the country. The doing of it would place her beyond her highest ambitions in her world of business, and make her a success in her chosen line beyond anything she had ever hoped.

But she shook her head, scarcely pausing to realize the magnitude of what was being offered to her.

"I could not do your work," she said in a clear firm voice. "Circumstances have changed with me, and your work would involve a letting down of standards that have suddenly become dear to me. Besides, I have no time. I am soon to be married, and I have a great deal to do. I shall have to decline your proposition."

As she turned from seeing her caller out, she noticed lying on a little table by the door a card with a newspaper clipping, a bit of a poem, pasted on it, and Ellen's name penciled below. "Dear Ellen! She must have come and left it here while I went to the firehouse!" She read the poem, her heart strangely stirred.

The angels from their thrones on high
Look down on us with wondering eye,
That where we are but passing guests
We build such strong and solid nests,
And where we hope to stay for aye
We scarce take pains one stone to lay!

Like a knife the little rhyme went through her heart. Ah! That was what she had been doing, building a house *here* for her*self*, when a mansion was being prepared for her in another country! And Ellen had seen her disloyalty, and had taken this quiet gentle way of trying to make her see what she was doing! Dear Ellen!

Suddenly she stepped over to the table in the window where lay all the blueprints and plans for the house she had meant to build, and with one motion of her arm she swept them all into the wastebasket! What were they to her now? She was going home with her bridegroom to dwell in the mansion he had prepared for her, and it would be far more perfect than any she could have designed for herself, because he had made it for her! Because he loved her! He had bought her life with his scarred face, his wounded hands and feet, even his shed blood!

She shuddered as she remembered the words of the fire chief.

Then with a swift bright look around the room, with all its careful appointments—the room that now seemed so transient and imperfect in the thought of the mansion she was soon to see—she went out to do her lord's bidding, for he had told her to watch and be ready for his coming, which might perhaps be today!

LIFE OUT OF DEATH

AFTERWARD Philip Gardley remembered his brother Stephen as he stood at the curb just a minute before it happened. What a pleasant smile had been on his face, and how tall and straight and handsome he had looked! The memory wrenched Philip's heart with a dull never-ceasing pain. Stephen had always been such a wonderful brother, more like a father than a brother to Philip, who could not remember his father.

It happened just after the brothers had completed an important conference arranging for Philip to enter into full partnership in the business which Stephen had built up into phenomenal prominence and success. Philip had finished a leisurely college education, topping it off with a prolonged European trip. They came out of the house together to drive down to the office in Stephen's car, which stood in front of their home. And Philip, seeing a girl across the street, called a greeting to her. He stepped out into the road the better to hear what she was saying, his Panama hat in hand, a smile on his lips, the honors of the partnership in the business resting lightly upon his irresponsible shoulders.

He glanced back as he stepped out into the road and caught that last glimpse of his brother standing on the curb with that look of quiet satisfaction upon his face, as if the thing he had just done meant the summit of his desire.

Even as Philip called out: "Just a minute, Steve," the idea touched the back of his mind a bit superficially: "Good old Steve! I believe this partnership means more to him than it does to me! He always was an unselfish fellow. I must buck up and take things more seriously!" He flung an easy smile behind him, and caught that last vivid impression.

Afterward nobody could describe how it happened. The street was broad and smooth, with plenty of room everywhere. There was no one in sight either way as Philip stepped out. An instant later a low-bodied, speedy sport car careened around the corner on two wheels and whirled madly toward him. Its twelve cylinders merely purred in the distance, and as it shot forward it gave no warning, sounded no horn. Only Stephen, standing on the curb, saw the onrushing danger. He gave one lunge forward and pushed his brother out of the way, but was struck himself and crushed by the heavy car as it sped wildly on and vanished around the next corner, its low-crouched driver taking no time to look back.

The girl across the street screamed and covered

her face with her hands. Philip, unaware of what had really happened, bruised and much shaken, highly indignant, gathered himself up to look toward that gallant figure of the brother who had stood smiling just a moment before, and found him gone! And down in the road at his feet lay a mangled, limp form with blood streaming from the face.

A crowd began to gather. The frightened mother rushed from the house and knelt in the road beside her son. Someone sent for the police and another sent for the ambulance. They telephoned a doctor, and the hospital. The hysterical girl on the sidewalk, and several neighbors who had witnessed the accident from afar, began to piece the story together. Telegraph wires grew hot with messages. Patrol wagons and motorcycles started on a chase for the automobile that had done the deed.

But Stephen Gardley lay white and still upon the bed in the dim hospital room with two doctors and several nurses hovering over him, a white, anguished mother kneeling by his side. And Philip Gardley, the boyish smile dead upon his stark set face, stood at the foot of the bed gripping the iron railing of the footboard, and watched his brother slowly dying in his stead.

For hours they waited there. It seemed like ages to the brother who had never in his life before had anything hard to bear. Minute by minute, hour after hour, Philip had to go over that scene, always beginning with that picture of his splendid, dependable brother standing there waiting for him with that smile of perfect contentment upon his lips.

He had to reconstruct everything that must have happened, to know all that had passed in his brother's mind in that one swift instant of comprehension and choice. It had to be one or the other of them, and Stephen had chosen to be the victim. There was not time to save them both! It was like Stephen to do it, of course. But considering all things, Philip recognized how much better it would have been for everyone if he had been the victim. Not better for himself! He shivered as he thought of himself lying there in pain with life slowly ebbing away. He had no conception of any such possibility for himself. Yet Stephen had unhesitatingly chosen death for himself, that he, Philip, irresponsible, selfish, might go on living. And he wasn't worth it! He knew in his heart that practically everyone, even his mother, would think so. Yet he had been left here to live, at such a cost, and Stephen had been struck down!

The awfulness of it all would roll over him overwhelmingly, till he longed to drop out of sight, out of existence, to call on the rocks and the mountains to hide him from the world that had so loved Stephen.

There was no phase of the terrible occurrence that did not force itself upon him as he stood there, on trembling limbs that threatened to crumple under him, gripping that white iron bar with hands that felt weak as water. It seemed that he grew ages older while he stood there watching that white face, swathed in bloodmarked bandages, those closed eyes, watching his mother's anguish, his own heart wrenched with the imminence of dreadful loss. How was he going to live without his brother?

All his life this brother had been safeguarding him, supplying him with what he needed, even fulfilling his every fancy, and how carelessly he had accepted it all! How as a matter of course he had taken it as only his due, and asked for more. Yes, and got it too! The expensive car, for instance! He had found afterward that the business was in straits just then and Stephen had had to drive a cheap secondhand car to manage the extra expense for him. And then his trip to Europe! And the partnership! Oh, the stabbing pain that shot through him at that thought! What would the business be with Stephen gone?

Oh, wasn't there something that could be done to save him even now?

Yet when he wildly sought the doctor in the hall and besieged him with questions, he only gravely shook his head, and sent him, desperate, back to grip that iron rail and watch for a possible flutter of those white eyelids. Oh, would there not be at least a word, a look, before he went from them forever?

And then, at last, it came—a look fully conscious, a slow smile of precious understanding and farewell that Philip would carry with him into eternity; a voice, low, vibrant, clear—Stephen's last words:

"It's all right, Phil. You'll carry on!"

A fleeting look of deep love into his mother's eyes, and he was gone!

Stephen was gone!

And he, Philip, was left to carry on!

How that thought came down upon his light and easy soul with crushing meaning! How the boy of a day ago shrank into himself and cried out in protest to a God he did not know. How he went through the interminable days of anguish that dragged themselves so unmercifully slowly until the funeral was over! His white, anguished face looked out as from the gloom of the valley of the shadow. People said, "How he loved him!" in slow astonished voices, and looked after him wonderingly. No one had thought that he had it in him to love and appreciate his brother so deeply.

But Philip did not hear them, did not see the surprise in their faces. He went the necessary way through those awful days up to the afternoon of the service in a kind of daze, seeing but one thought ever before him. He, Philip, would have been a dead man, if Stephen had not died for him! There had been no other possibility! Stephen had chosen to lay his splendid, successful life down in his place! Stephen had died that he might live, and therefore it was his place henceforth to die to himself that he might live Stephen's life for him. Stephen was an infinitely better man than Philip knew he ever could be, and now that Stephen was gone and the world could not see him nor know him anymore, it was his place to carry on Stephen's life as he had begun it, and it seemed an appalling thing that he was asked to do.

The day of the service, Philip sat by his mother, where she had chosen to stay, close by the casket where lay that sweet, strong face.

When Philip lifted his grief-filled eyes, there across the room sat Enid Ainsley, the pretty girl to whom he had been speaking when the accident occurred. He remembered how she had called some nothing across that had made him step nearer to hear her. Perhaps there had been a bit of self-consciousness on his own part as he moved toward her, because he knew that Stephen and his mother did not approve of his friendship with Enid. Yes, he knew that there was a fascination about her. He had owned to himself more than once that he was in love with her; yet now in the revulsion that this catastrophe had brought, she seemed almost an offense sitting there in her becoming costume of deep black. He could not bear to look at her. She seemed the cause of his great loss. He wished she had not come. Why should she weep in that hysterical way? It seemed to him that good taste should have kept her away.

Ah! She was one of the things that must be cut out of his life from henceforth. Stephen would never have hung around with a girl like Enid.

Yet even as he turned his eyes from looking at the girl, it came to him that Stephen would never have felt resentment toward her. He was always full of kindliness even toward those who had injured him.

And of course it was not Enid's fault that he had been standing there in the middle of the road talking to her when the peril came.

He groaned in spirit as the interminable service dragged along. He heard nothing of the comfort it was meant to give. He was thinking of his own lost life, thinking how he must now fit himself into his brother's place and live his life instead of his own.

He had no impatience toward this idea, no question but that of course he would do it. There was no

question as to whether he would shirk this most un-
congenial task. It was something that his inner nature demanded of him. It was just that his own
bright, thoughtless life was dead, ended as thoroughly as if he had been crushed beside his brother
there on the street by the murderous car; and he had
entered into the life of another to live it out.

There might be a time when he could look back
and be glad of the splendid foundation which his
brother had laid for him to build upon, the best start
possible that a young man could have in life. At
present he could only be aghast.

He looked at the beautiful dead face in the coffin
with a stern mask upon his own, struggling to keep
his inner feelings from being seen by the world, for
it seemed he was really looking upon his own face
lying there among the flowers. He, Philip Gardley,
dead with his brother! He knew he could never be
his brother, much as he should try, and yet he must
try, and equally he could not be himself because of
trying.

The first night after the funeral was agony.
Stephen's room empty! He could just remember how
when he was a little boy Stephen was away at college for four long years. He seemed a great stranger-
hero when he came back. But now it had been so
very long that Stephen had been at home. Grammar
school days and high school days and then college for
himself, and always that wonderful older brother at
home making things go, as his father would have
done if he had lived. Why, it hadn't occurred to him

that Stephen could ever die, at least not till he him-self was an old, old man. Old man! Ah! He drew in his breath sharply. Would he have to live out that long, long life for Stephen? "Carry on!" Those were his last words! It seemed so interminable to Philip, lying in his bed, with Stephen's room closed, empty. No Stephen in the house, ever, anymore. He was to be Stephen now! Incredible thought!

He knew his mother was feeling the emptiness of the house, the agony of loss, too. Her door across the hall stood open. He could hear a soft sob now and then, quickly suppressed.

Stephen would have gone to comfort her if he had been here. He had always been like that. He could dimly remember Stephen comforting his mother when he was a tiny child; it must have been after his father's death, although he could not remember that.

Well, if he was to carry on, it was his place now to comfort his mother. Could he do it? He shrank from it inexpressibly. He doubted if he could. She had al-ways comforted him—when Stephen wasn't there to do it. But now he was in Stephen's place and must not let her see how much he needed comfort himself. How old he felt!

He lay there trying to get the consent of himself to go and try to do what Stephen would have done; trying to imagine how one should go about com-forting a mother; trying to fall asleep before he had actually decided if he must. But by and by his con-science, or something that answered for conscience in his hitherto carefree soul, prodded him beyond the limits and he stumbled up and across the hall, entering his mother's room almost stealthily, as if he might change his mind after all.

She had ceased sobbing. Perhaps she was asleep and it was not necessary. He could see the outline of her head on the pillow; her frail arm beneath the lacy sleeve was lifted, holding a handkerchief to her eyes. Then she gave a soft convulsive breath as of a suppressed moan, and his conscience drove him across the floor, while his soul was suggesting that his mother would probably think it odd of him to come.

She looked up as he approached the bed, half startled. The thought menaced him that perhaps she would not want him. Perhaps she even looked upon him as the cause of her beloved elder son's death, just as he had thought of that girl. Perhaps his mother shrank from him, and could not love him as she had. The thought went like a sword through his newly awakened soul, and twisted about painfully. He was standing over her now. Perhaps he should not have come. He felt abject. Should he go back? But he could not do that without saying something.

He dropped upon his knee beside the bed, bent over her, and felt his own tears start like a child. He wanted to hide his face in her neck and weep, tell her he could not carry on, ask her to comfort him as she had always done.

But he was a man! He could not do that! He was to *carry on!*

Blindly he groped with his lips and touched her eyelids, wet with tears, and then was stung with the thought that Stephen had always kissed her so, on her eyelids, and now he was taking Stephen's place. Oh, he ought not to have done that! Perhaps it would hurt her! What an everlasting blunderer he was! He could never learn to take Stephen's place without hurting. He couldn't be Stephen no matter how he tried! Stephen would not have done a tactless thing like that. He should have kissed her forehead as he had always done, lightly, or her lips. But no, he had to kiss her eyelids, the very thing that would remind her most of her loss! He wanted to turn and run away to hide in dismay at himself.

But the mother's arm suddenly went around him gently, and she reached her lips to his and murmured: "Philip! Dear son!" and Philip stole away again awkwardly, embarrassedly. He had done his best, and perhaps she liked it. She seemed to him as usual, yet somehow he knew he had not comforted her, only showed her that he was sorry and that he needed comfort himself. Stephen would have had words about heaven and hereafter. Stephen was that way. Philip groped around in his mind for some form of family tradition called religion that would help now, but nothing came to mind. Heaven seemed very far away and undesirable. One had to go on living and being somebody else. All the brightness of life was gone. He had to carry on for someone else.

He went down to the office in the morning with a heavy heart and a stern face. He called his brother's helpers about him and tried to gather up the threads that had been dropped by the head of the establishment, but though he conscientiously sought to understand, and asked many questions most earnestly, his mind seemed a blank. There was something hard and artificial about all that he did. He found himself trying to look older than he was, to appear as Stephen would have appeared.

"He's doin' the best he can," said the old Scotsman who had looked after the building since Stephen was first in business. "He's tryin' hard, but a body can't take the place o' thot mon. *Nae* body can!"

And, although the Scotsman did not know it, Philip heard him, gave him one keen glance, and went back to his office to drop his head upon his desk and groan in spirit. How could he carry on for Stephen? What could he do? What was lacking?

Day after day went by and his heart grew heavier. How could he keep it up? He went gravely from house to office and back again, going through the duties of each day carefully, precisely, becoming more proficient in their technique each day, yet getting no nearer to his goal. When strangers from out of town came in to do business they sought out the old helpers instead of the new head. They were missing Stephen and he could do nothing about it. He was making a miserable failure of it all! He was not taking Stephen's place even to his mother. He knew it. He was just Philip, the younger son, and she was grieving alone for Stephen, her dependence!

His mother roused to alarm at last, urged him to go out among his young friends, invite them home, bring some brightness about the house. But he shook his head.

"No, Mother, I couldn't. I'm done with all that!" he answered gravely to her pleading.

The circle of his friends talked him over.

"He might as well have died," said a young girl bitterly. "He's just like one dead. Or like a stranger! He looks at you from so far away! Whoever would have thought his brother's death would have made him like this? He can't bring Stephen back by acting like the tomb!"

And one day he heard two elderly men conversing. They did not know their voices carried to the seat behind them in the suburban train.

"Yes, he's settled down more than I ever dreamed he could," said one, a noted lawyer, whom he knew as a dear friend of his dead father. "I'm sure he's going to make a good man. He used to be a bit wild, but he seems to have given all that up. But he'll never be half the man his brother Stephen was!"

"Oh, no!" said the other who was a wealthy businessman and also an officer in the church he and his mother attended. "He lacks something. I wouldn't exactly say pep! He's taken hold of his business with a stern rigidity I wouldn't have expected of one so unstable as he was, but he lacks that deep vital spark that Stephen had, that was almost spirituality, even in business matters."

"Yes," said the lawyer thoughtfully, "Stephen was the most godlike man I ever knew. For so young a man it was most remarkable. It was almost as if Christ were come down and living his life for him. He fairly radiated God in his whole contact with the world."

Philip sat listening behind his sheltering newspaper and let the thought drive deep into his heart.

It carried real conviction with it. That was the matter with him. He was not godlike. Stephen had been godlike and he never could be. He was sure of that! It wasn't in him. Yet somehow, if he knew how to go about it, he would like to try.

When a mere boy in his teens he had joined the church. In a general way he had known himself for a sinner and admitted belief in the atoning sacrifice of the Savior. It seemed a kind benevolent thing for the Savior to have done to die on the cross in a general atonement, and he always felt that if there was some mistake about it and it should prove not to be true, it was at least "a peach of a fake," and a pleasant way to get through life to have a safe feeling about the hereafter. But he had scarcely given two thoughts to the matter since he united with the church. He felt that he had done all that was necessary. There remained but to live a fairly decent life and he would be eligible for any crowns that were to be handed out. Now, however, as he thought of Stephen and of what these two respected men had been saying, he saw that there must be something more. Stephen had been godlike. Well, then *he* would be godlike too! He would get to work and get for himself some real righteousness such as Stephen had.

To that end he suggested to his mother that they go to prayer meeting that night. Much surprised, she assented and they went, but he got very little help from that save a mild kind of self-satisfaction that he had gone. An old deacon took the service and droned out worn platitudes that did not reach beyond the surface.

But there was mention of a new leader for the Boy Scouts, as the old leader had resigned, and volunteers were called for. Philip thought it over and offered his own services. Perhaps this was the way to become godlike, to make himself what Stephen had been and make his life count for the things that had meant so much to Stephen.

They told him that a Sunday school class of boys went with the Scout organization, and after a moment's hesitation he took that over too. This was what Stephen would have been likely to do.

He wondered what he should teach those boys. He prepared some platitudes and realized hopelessly the boys' restlessness. The empty words he was giving them meant nothing, had no aim. They were letting them roll off their well-armored young souls like a shower of harmless shot. He wasn't getting anywhere. They didn't even like him very well. He could see that.

For weeks he went on dragging himself through duties, financial and spiritual, getting nowhere. Each week when a meeting was over he resolved to resign before the next, yet went on for Stephen's sake.

Someone asked him to address the Sunday school on Boys' Day because Stephen had always had such a wonderful message for the boys. He tried to do it, but saw through their politeness how bored they were. He had nothing to give them but more platitudes that they already knew by heart. He was really giving them some of the same old dry phrases he had hated so in speakers when he was a boy.

That night he got down upon his knees and wept in the dark. He actually spoke to God and told him he was a failure; that he couldn't go on any longer; that God, if there was a God who expected him to carry on, must help! He couldn't do another thing alone!

And then, almost as an answer, there came the idea of going to the minister for help. The minister had never struck him as being a man to whom one could easily go in trouble. He was a conservative, elderly, rather formal man; but a minister *ought* to be able to help in a case like this, oughtn't he? He was supposed to help the soul to God, wasn't he? And Stephen had always respected him.

So, late at night, almost midnight it was, he took his hat and went out, walking down the street on what to him seemed a very hopeless errand. But it was a last resort.

A stranger opened the door, a younger man than the minister, a man with disarming eyes and a burr on his tongue that came from across the water. Philip liked him. His eyes had something in them that reminded him of Stephen.

The stranger explained that the minister had gone out to see a dying man and he was waiting up for him. He said the minister might be back soon, and opened the door with such a friendly warmth that Philip stepped in, wondering at himself for doing it.

He was not in a mood for talking with strangers, and the minister would not want to be kept up any longer after he got home. He should have waited until another time. When he was inside he said so, intending to go home at once. But the stranger, who said his name was McKnight, looked at him with that disarming smile and said:

"Is there anything that I could do for you? I am a servant of the Lord Jesus also, and shall be glad if there is any way that I can help you."

Philip never knew how it came about. Certainly he had no intention of taking that stranger into his confidence. But he found himself sitting in the cozy library telling this man with the holy eyes just what was happening in his life and how unhappy he was.

Just a few questions and the kindly stranger, who had amazingly become a friend, had the whole story of Philip's life.

"And so, my friend," said the stranger, "your brother was a man who knew the Lord Jesus, and had the power of the resurrection in his life. And you are trying to be your brother without knowing his Lord or having the right to that power! Is that it?"

"I don't know what you mean by the resurrection power," said Philip.

"The resurrection power is the life Christ brought from the tomb when he rose from the dead," answered McKnight. "It is his life that came out of death—'the life whereby Jesus conquered death.' If you have that power within you, it will enable you to live a life on a higher plane than ordinary living. You want to be godlike? There is no other power that can make you show forth the God-Man Christ Jesus but the power of his resurrection."

"That's all Greek to me," said Philip with bewildered eyes. "I never learned the language you are speaking."

"Well, I'll put it more simply," said the stranger. "You can't be like a man unless you know him, can you?"

"You can't even if you do know him," said Philip sadly. "I've known my brother all my life, and I've tried my best to be like him, and let his life go on in me, and I find it can't be done."

"But are you quite sure that you knew him?" asked the keen-eyed questioner. "You have found something about him into which you cannot enter, his godlikeness that people speak of. Did you ever know your brother in this phase of his experience? Did you ever get to know thoroughly his inmost heart on this matter?"

Philip stared, then answered quickly: "No, I wouldn't let him talk to me about religious matters. I wasn't interested."

"Exactly. Then how could you know him thoroughly, and how could you be like him in that respect if you never went with him through his deepest experiences?"

"I suppose I couldn't," said Philip hopelessly. "Then you think there's no use?"

"No! Oh no! I think there is great use. It is quite true that your *brother's* life can never go on in you, but you *can* know his Christ, who made your brother godlike. The Lord Jesus Christ is willing to live his resurrection life through you, if you will, as much as he ever did through your brother. That is a miracle, of course, but we are speaking of heavenly things, you see."

"How could one know Christ?" Philip's tone was full of awe.

"The first step is to accept him as your own personal Savior. When you do that his Spirit takes up his dwelling in you. Then surrender to him so utterly that you actually reckon your self-life to have died with him on the cross, so that you can say: 'I am crucified with Christ: nevertheless I live; yet not I, but Christ liveth in me: and the life which I now live in the flesh I live by the faith of the Son of God, who loved me, and gave himself for me.' Isn't that substantially the same thing that you have been trying to do for your brother, to die to your own life so that the life of your brother might go on in the same channels it had when he was living?"

"It is," said Philip with dawning comprehension.

"Well, that's all, only put Christ in your brother's place. It is *Christ* whose life must go on through yours; for I am sure that is what happened in your brother's life. It was Christ who was living in him, not Stephen Gardley. And when his body was crushed it was Christ whose resurrection power was hindered, through having one less human life to dwell in. Did it ever occur to you that the Lord Jesus can be seen today only through men and women who are willing to have self slain with all its old programs, standards, ambitions, desires, aims, will, and let Christ take up his abode in them? The world saw Jesus through your brother because your brother counted himself as crucified with him, and was therefore under that promise in Romans 6: 'For if we have been planted together in the likeness of his death, we shall be also in the likeness of his resurrection. . . . Likewise reckon ye also yourselves to be dead indeed unto sin but alive unto God through Jesus Christ our Lord.' You see, my friend, the death and resurrection of Christ is the power of God, and you have a right to it in your life if you are willing for this death-union with Christ himself.

"But it is not to be acquired by any effort of your own. It is only through the death of self that he can come in. There is not room for him and you both, and the natural man must go because God can do nothing with him. The old sinful nature cannot inherit the kingdom of heaven."

Philip listened in wonder as the way was made plain. He was deeply moved at the stranger's prayer for him, and finally went home to read his Bible.

McKnight had sent him to the story of the crucifixion, and straight through the four Gospels he read it, till the scene was printed as vividly on his mind as the death of his own brother. For the first time since Stephen's death, Philip lost sight of that bloodstained face lying in the dust of the road, and saw his Savior hanging on the cross instead. He felt the shame, the scoffs, the insults, quivered at the nails driven in the tender hands and feet, saw the trickling blood from the thorn-crown, the awful spear thrust!

Ah! This was the one who had died that he might live *eternally!* And this King of all the earth wanted to live out his life through him! He was asked to "carry on" for the Savior of the world!

It was just before daybreak that he turned out his light and knelt beside his open window with the morning star still shining, the dawn creeping softly into the sky, and surrendered to his risen Lord; confessed all his own unworthiness, his vain efforts of the flesh to be like another *man;* laid down himself to die with his Lord and said: "I am crucified with thee, Lord Jesus. Nevertheless I live, yet not I, Philip Gardley, but Christ liveth *in* me, and the life which I now live in the flesh I live by the faith of the Son of God, who loved me, and gave himself for me!"

Then a new day began.

He went downstairs to breakfast with a different look in his face. He bent over his anxious mother tenderly and kissed her. He said:

"Mother, I've found the Lord Jesus, and it's going to be all different now!"

They began to feel it almost at once in the office, and as the days went by.

"That young man is growing like his brother!" one of the office force said.

"He is growing like Jesus Christ!" said an old friend of his father's who happened to be in the office at the time.

"Well, I suppose you're right," said the first. "That was really what I meant, I guess!" and his voice had a note of awe in it.

But then because the enemy never lets a chance go by to hinder a newborn soul, Enid Ainsley came into his life again.

Someone had asked her into the church choir for a special musical festival, for she had a really marvelous voice and was besides quite decorative, with her gold hair, her vivid complexion, and her great blue eyes. Philip also had promised to help with the music and Enid managed it quite easily that he should take her home from the rehearsals.

At first he treated her gravely, pleading business and hurrying away at once. but soon she inveigled him into her home and tried to bring back the old free and easy camaraderie.

She played her part cleverly, leading him on to almost hope that perhaps she too was changing.

One night he tried to tell her of his own experience and the new hope that had come into his life. But she flung away from him.

"Oh, for pity's sake, Phil, aren't you ever going to be yourself again?" she cried out impatiently.

"I hope not," he said gravely.

"Well, I think it's silly, this trying to be like your brother! It was well enough to respect his memory for awhile and all that, but it gets boring to keep it up. For heaven's sake, snap out of it, and quickly, too."

"I'm not trying to be like my brother any longer," he said quietly. "I found it was impossible, because, you know, it wasn't he who was living in him, it was another."

"What do you mean?"

"I mean the Lord Jesus Christ."

"For heaven's sake!" she turned upon him. "Are you turning religious? Phil Gardley gone religious! Well, that's a great joke. That's *precious!* I'll have to tell the gang."

"No," said Philip steadily. "Philip Gardley hasn't gone religious. Philip Gardley has died! Christ who died for me is living his life in me. Henceforth it's not to be my life, but his. Enid, this thing is very real to me. It's not a joke. And Enid, I want you to let me tell you about it. I want you to know him too. Enid, I've been loving you for a long time—"

Then Enid used all her guiles to turn his attention to herself and his love for her.

But Philip gently brought back the subject again and again, urging her to accept his Lord also, until at last she flouted out upon him with a cold hard look on her lovely face.

"I'm tired of this," she said haughtily. "I don't care to share your love with anyone else, even *God!* You can choose between us. Either you give up this fanatical nonsense or I'm done with you once and for all."

He pleaded with her. He tried to make her understand that the thing had been *done.* That he was no longer in a position to choose. He had died with Christ on that cross long ago! He had given his word! But she only turned from him coldly; and at last he went away, sadly, with a break in his heart.

At home he knelt before his Lord and struggled

long. Was earthly love to be denied him? Why could not this beautiful woman be drawn by God's Spirit to love his Lord?

It was a long hard struggle, his will against God's will. But was that dying with Christ? He was startled at the thought.

Worn with the struggle, he flung himself upon his bed, and sharply the words of the young Scotsman came back to him:

"It is just in the measure that the 'I' has been crucified in your life, that Christ in the power of his resurrection can be revealed to the world through you."

Torn between his desire to have his own way, and his growing realization of what it might mean to his Christian witness if he married this girl, he dropped finally into an uneasy sleep. His last thought was a prayer that God would somehow make Enid what she ought to be, and give her to him.

And then there came to him a vision of Christ, standing there at the foot of his bed, with the print of the nails in his hands, and the thorns upon his brow, looking deep into Philip Gardley's soul.

"You and I died on Calvary together, Philip," he said. "Are you remembering that? And now, if I give you what you are asking for, this girl will come between you and me! Are you prepared for that? Are you *willing* for that? She belongs to the world and cares only for the things of the world. She will not accept me as her Savior! You will have to choose between us as she has said. You may have your way if you will, but you must understand that it will lead you through distress and sorrow, and although I shall never cease to love you, it will separate you and me in our walk together. It will also prevent you from showing my resurrection power to the world. The world will not be able to see me through you if you choose this way. Can you not trust me that this is not best for you?"

He awoke startled, and the struggle went on, but at last he yielded, kneeling low before his Lord and crying out:

At thy feet I fall,
Yield thee up my all,
To suffer, live or die,
For my Lord crucified.

Out into the world he went, a different world, where a closed door had utterly changed his course. And one day he found a bit of a poem in a magazine, lying on a desk in a room where he had to wait for an interview:

Is there some door closed by the Father's hand,
  Which widely open you had hoped to see?
Trust God, and wait—for when he shuts the door
  He keeps the key!

The days went by and strange things followed. Disaster suddenly surrounded him on every hand. The bank closed that held his financial situation in its grasp. The business went to the wall and he had to begin all over again. There were perils and perplexities everywhere. But still his Christian witness grew brighter. People marveled at the way he took his testings. He was walking through it all in the daily consciousness of Christ as his constant companion. He was able to say as the days went by, each bringing its new problem:

I do not ask my cross to understand,
  My way to see;
Better in darkness just to feel thy hand
  And follow thee.

There came a Sunday when he sat in a shadowed seat back under the gallery of the Sunday school room during the review of the Sunday school lesson by the superintendent. Suddenly the superintendent asked a question.

"Children, did any of you ever see anybody who made you think of Jesus Christ? Who seemed like what you would expect of Jesus Christ if he were to come back here in visible form?"

A quick eager hand went up, Jimmy Belden, one of Philip's Boy Scouts.

"Well, Jimmy?" said the superintendent.

Jimmy stood up promptly and in a clear voice said, "Mr. Philip Gardley!"

Then did Philip Gardley bow his head and cover his eyes with his hand, his heart filled with glad humility. God had given him that great honor and privilege of being able to show Christ in some small measure at least, to that one Boy Scout, and perhaps to give him some little idea of what that life was whereby Jesus conquered death! It thrilled him with a joy inexpressible and brought tears of humility to his eyes.

And that night as he stood by his window looking up to the stars and thought of it all, his heart recalled a verse he had read that day:

He was better to me than all my hopes,
  Better than all my fears,
He made a bridge of my broken works,
  And a rainbow of my tears.
The billows that guarded my sea-girt path
  But bore my Lord on their crest!
When I dwell on the days of my wilderness march
  I can lean on his love and rest!

THE
MINISTER'S SON

FAITH Holden arrived at her sister Myra's home about the middle of the afternoon, after a three years' stay abroad. She was welcomed joyously by the entire family, including her minister brother-in-law, and the seven children, of whom Joy, aged ten, was the youngest, and Barry, aged nineteen, the oldest. In between there were Rosalie, John, the twins Jean and Joan, and Steve.

They welcomed their guest so eagerly that it was some minutes before they realized that they had not yet taken her into the house. Then they roused to their duties and escorted her upstairs to the guest room, and one by one drifted away to their various interests, leaving the two sisters alone for a good long talk, the kind of talk that people who love one another, and have been separated for a long time, do enjoy so much.

Faith settled down in the big winged chair by the

window, where she could watch the changes that had come in her sister's plump, contented face.

"And now tell me all about everything!" she said. "It's easy to see you are well and happy." She laughed.

Then followed the details of all that had only been touched upon in letters, details that made the past live again.

At last the elder sister rose.

"I'm talking you to death and you ought to rest, Faith. For, you know, I have a plan for this evening. I'm hoping you'll feel you can go to a meeting with us tonight! We're having such a wonderful evangelist. He's been with us in the church for three weeks and this is his last week. I was so glad when I found you would get here before he leaves. He has taken the town by storm. They even close the shops for an hour in the afternoon because everybody wants to go to the afternoon meeting. Do you think you'll be too tired to go?"

"Why, of course not, Myra. I'll be as eager to hear him as you are to have me. And the children? Do they all go out to the meeting? Nobody has to stay at home with them? As I remember it they were all Christians when I left, except the two youngest. Have they come into the fold?"

"Oh, yes, they're all church members. Our little Joy united at the last communion, and she's very much interested in her Sunday school class, and the catechism class and all. She and Steve have been quite prominent in the children's meetings we've been having in connection with the evangelistic campaign. They go out after school and distribute Gospels and tracts and invitations, and they've brought all their school friends to the meetings. No, nobody has to stay at home with them. They are all deeply interested and working in the meetings. That is, all except Barry."

The mother sighed and looked troubled.

"Except *Barry?*" said the aunt. "Why, I thought I remembered Barry as being a very remarkable young Christian when he was just a little fellow!"

"Yes, he was," said the mother, knitting her brows and giving another sigh, "but somehow he's got switched off the track. No, it's not college. He goes to a strictly fundamental college, and he's well taught. I don't think he has any doubts at all about the great truths of Christianity. He never has expressed any. He just isn't interested, that's all, and when you try to talk to him about it he looks at you in a strange way and says what you're saying is a lot of 'hooey.' It's the strangest thing! Once I pressed him hard to tell me what was the matter, and his answer was, 'Well I can't see it, that's all. Nobody is sincere! It's all a lot of baloney!' "

"Sincere?" said his aunt, startled. "With such a wonderful father and mother!"

"That's it!" said his mother earnestly. "Not that I'm anything, but he has such a wonderful father. He surely must see that! Of course his father says this is just a phase, and he'll outgrow it. I'm sure I hope he will. It's terribly distressing. You see, he doesn't go to church anymore, and that's *so* mortifying when his father is the minister!"

"Doesn't go to church?" said Aunt Faith, aghast.

"No," said Barry's mother, "I don't believe he's been inside the church for more than a year. We've coaxed and done everything we know how to do. We've even tried to bribe him to go again, but it doesn't do a bit of good. He just shuts his lips tight and something hard glints in his eyes, and he says, *'No.'* His father even offered to make a good big down-payment on a new car for him if he would go to church for a year, but he said no, he'd get his own car! And he *did!* I am sure I don't know where he goes instead of church, but he's never there anymore."

There were tears in her eyes as she looked up sorrowfully.

"Then he hasn't heard this wonderful evangelist speak at all!"

"No, he hasn't heard him! The night we had him here to dinner hoping he'd get acquainted with Barry, Barry didn't come home at all until way after midnight!"

"Oh!" said Aunt Faith softly, pitifully. "That's so sad. I can't realize that is possible. I'm sure Barry was saved when he was a child! How he used to love to hear the Bible stories, and how earnestly he prayed! Oh, I'm sure he was saved. And when once a soul is saved, God never lets go of his own, you know. We'll have to get together regularly every day, you and I, and make it a special subject of prayer. He's a child of the faith! He'll come back. We'll *pray*. Of course you and John have been praying, I know, but we'll pray together. We'll take that verse, '... if two of you shall agree on earth as touching anything that they shall ask, it shall be done for them....' I have great faith in that promise."

Barry's mother gave her sister a startled look.

"I've prayed, yes, but I really haven't had much faith lately. I'm afraid Barry's just grown up and got away from God. Of course his father is quite sure we needn't worry. He says Barry will come back into church work someday. But I don't know, I'm sure!" and she sighed again.

"When did he begin to get this way?" asked the aunt thoughtfully. "What was the cause?"

"I'm sure I don't know. He just began criticizing Christians, that was all. We reprimanded him, of course, but he only laughed. He said it was all bunk what they said, that they didn't live up to what they preached. As nearly as I can remember he came in one day and told his father that the senior elder was a liar. He said he told one man something and then told another the exact opposite. His father told him that of course he just didn't understand, and he must never talk that way about a good man again. 'Good man, my eye!' said Barry, 'If he's a good man, lead me from him. He's a *liar!*' And then a few days later he came and told me the president of the women's missionary society was an old hypocrite. I said, 'Oh, Barry! Remember what your father said!' And he said, 'You just ought to hear her talk to her milkman! You'd see what I mean.' There! There he comes now. Don't let him know we've been talking about him!"

And then they could hear Barry come whistling up the stairs. He came and stood in his aunt's doorway, leaning against the door frame, beaming.

"Oh, say! Aunt Faith, it's good to have you back again!" he said. "I've missed you a lot. You and I used to be great pals, didn't we?"

"We did." His aunt laughed tenderly. "And you don't know how I missed you. Do you know, Barry, I always felt that you prolonged my youth ten years at least. You were as good company as a grown person."

"Well," said Barry earnestly. "I'll say you were a wonderful friend for a kid to have! I'll never forget all you did for me. All those picture puzzles you got for me, real grown-up ones, and taught me how to put them together, watching colors and forms! And then all those stone blocks you bought, six whole boxes! And helped me to build bridges and railroad stations and towers and churches and bungalows. I'm in an architect's office this summer, and doing real well, they tell me, and I believe it was you who gave me my bent for architecture. Do you know, I've got all those blocks yet, and I love every one of them, especially those little blue slates for the roof. Got them locked in my closet. Of course I did let the kids play with them for a while till I found Joy biting her teeth through on some of them; she had taken little nicks out of their nice sharp edges. And then one day

I found Steve had built a castle out of them in his goldfish bowl, and the water was disintegrating them, so I took 'em away. I had to send to the manufacturer to replace some of them, but I've got them all now, every one, put away in the box according to the picture on the cover. And by the way, that was the cleverest way to make a kid pick up his toys! Why, I loved to put 'em away in the box according to the picture, as well as I did to get them out to build. Say, I'd like to build a bungalow now!"

"Why, so would I, Barry," said Aunt Faith with a twinkle of appreciation. "Let's do it while I'm here!"

"All right, that's a bargain!" said Barry. "How about tomorrow afternoon? I'll get home early from the office and we can work awhile before dinner. You never can do anything in the evenings in this house anymore. *Every*body goes to church!" He laughed almost bitterly.

Suddenly his mother spoke up: "And by the way, Barry, I wonder if you wouldn't like to take Aunt Faith over to the meeting tonight? She wants to go, and I have to run around to see Mrs. Parsons after dinner. She fell downstairs last night and broke her leg and she's sent for me. She wants me to take a notice for the Ladies' Aid to be given out in the meeting tonight. Rosalie and the twins have to go to the hotel to bring some girls to the meeting; and you can't depend on the rest, they have Junior Choir practice. I thought your aunt wouldn't want to go too early after her long journey. Will you take her?"

Barry looked up with a frown and a whimsical expression, as if his eyes were understanding more than his mother expected him to. He straightened up and looked at his mother. Was this another scheme to get him to go to church? And was Aunt Faith in it too? Then he looked quickly at his aunt.

But Aunt Faith looked up with a protest.

"No, Barry, don't you *think* of it!" she said quickly before he could answer his mother. "I haven't been away so long that I have forgotten the way to the church, and I'm not at all shy about going in alone. Don't change any of your plans for the evening on my account, please. I would feel most uncomfortable to have you do so."

And all the time behind Barry's back Barry's mother was signaling frantically with appealing eyes and shaking her head, but Aunt Faith finished her protest in spite of it.

"Barry, really, I mean it. I don't want one of you children to change any of your plans for me. I don't want to be a nuisance!"

Barry's face relaxed.

"Why, Aunt Faith, you *couldn't* be a nuisance!" he said. "Sure I'll take you to church if you want to go. Do you still like to sit in the gallery?"

"I adore it!" said Aunt Faith with a twinkle.

"All right, I'll get you the first seat in the synagogue. I suppose you want to see the whole show, don't you? Well, we'll go early. I'll take you down in my flivver."

Then with a smile he turned and strode past his astonished mother, down to the telephone in the lower hall. A moment later his mother, hurrying downstairs to look after some dinner arrangements, heard Barry at the telephone calling off a date with a girl!

She hustled right up the back stairs to her sister's room.

"Faith, you aren't asleep yet, are you? Isn't it *wonderful* that Barry's going to church! Now you'll be sure to get a good chance to work on him, won't you? Make him see how badly he's been treating us, how mortifying it is for the minister's son to stay away from church this way when the whole town is present."

"Oh, I wouldn't think that was nice, would you, Myra?" said Aunt Faith. "I'm sure he wouldn't care to come again if I began to lambast him about it the first thing. You just pray about it, Myra dear, and I will, and let us leave the rest to the Lord! The Holy Spirit knows how to bring conviction to his soul better than you and I do."

"Oh, but I think he ought to be made to see that he should go to church for *our* sakes, even if he isn't interested for his own, don't you?"

"Why, no," said the sister, "I don't know that I do. That wouldn't attain the real end for which you are anxious, would it? You want him to come because he desires to please the Lord, not *us*, don't you?"

"Oh, well, of course he would come to that," said the worried mother, "if he only would just get into things and hear what goes on. How can he expect to be interested if he doesn't hear anything? He needs to see how others are taking hold of this work. He needs to understand how popular this young preacher is."

"I'm not so sure," said Aunt Faith gravely. "Of course those influences do help in many instances, but it is something deeper than that we want, isn't it? We want him to come back to God, to get into communion with him, to go to church to worship him. I really don't believe just urging people to go to a meeting for your sake is going to help much. Nobody can come to God in the first place unless the Holy Spirit draws him. Nobody can come back to God when he has wandered away unless the Holy Spirit draws him. Only then can a soul really *want* God, you know."

"But don't you think Barry ought to come out of respect to his father?"

"Undoubtedly he ought, but that isn't the main thing. He ought to come out of respect to God. He ought to come to get near his Savior!"

"Oh, yes, of course," said Barry's mother anxiously. "But surely, Faith, you believe in inviting people to meetings?"

"Why, of course," said Aunt Faith, "*invite*, but not insist, not nag. Barry seems to be going of his own free will tonight. It may be only because he wants to be polite to me. But I should think our part was to pray that the Holy Spirit may open his heart to receive what he hears, and that you and I and the rest of us Christians shall not hinder the work of the Holy Spirit by anything in us that is awry."

"*Hinder?*" said the mother. "How could we hinder

the work of the Holy Spirit in Barry's life?"

"Well, I wouldn't be expected to know, would I?" said Aunt Faith. "But let's pray that if there is anything in us that is hindering, that God will open our eyes to it, shall we?"

"Why, of course," said the minister's wife a little stiffly, as if she were promising something utterly unnecessary. "But, Faith, if you get a good *chance*, you *will* speak to Barry, won't you? You know I've been depending on you to bring Barry to his senses."

"Well," smiled Faith, "if I were you I'd stop depending on me and begin to depend entirely on the Holy Spirit."

"You dear old sermonizer!" exclaimed her sister, suddenly coming up and kissing her again. "You always did live in the clouds, didn't you? Now, you lie down and get a good nap before the dinner bell rings! We have to have dinner exactly at six, you know, because the children go to the young people's choir practice at quarter before seven, and it makes everything so hurried if we are not on time."

But Faith Holden did not lie down for a nap immediately. Instead she locked her door and knelt down by her bed to pray for Barry.

Dinner was a hurried affair. Everybody was anxious to be off. Each one felt that his business was the most important. They all wanted to be waited on first, and then each wanted a second helping before the father had quite got around the first time. Then they all clamored for their dessert. But at last they all hastened away to their various engagements, till only Barry and Aunt Faith were left.

Barry was embarrassed. He thought they weren't treating Aunt Faith very well this first night of her homecoming.

"They're all so terribly busy!" he said apologetically. "Even the kid thinks the whole universe rests on her shoulders." But Aunt Faith only smiled and gave Barry another piece of pie and another cup of coffee.

"Oh, Barry," she said, "it's great to be sitting here looking at you, and you almost a man. It seems just the other day that you were born. I remember the first time I ever saw you. You were just eight days old. The nurse brought you to me and said, 'Here! Take this young man and get him to sleep! I've got to go down in the kitchen and get his mother something to eat.' And you stared up at me as if you were saying: 'Hello! You're somebody new, aren't you?' And I said, 'Yes, I'm somebody new, and we're going to have a grand time together.' And you stared on as if you were saying, 'You're somebody, and I'm somebody all by myself.' And I said, 'Yes, and now let's go look at the pictures on the wall. That's your grandmother in that big gold frame up there. She's a good scout. She'll make gingerbread men with currant eyes for you. Um-m! You'll like her! And that's your grandfather in that next frame. He's a good scout too! He'll ride you on his foot. You'll like that! And there in the next frames are your great grandmother and your great grandfather. You'll like them. And here on this wall are your aunts and uncles. Oh you'll have a grand time with them! Uncle John, and Uncle Rand, and Uncle Sam, and Uncle

Will, and Aunt Emily and Aunt Mary and Aunt Sue
and Aunt Carolyn. They're swell persons. And over
on this wall are all your cousins, Emmy Lou and
Betty and Jane and Lynne and Fred and Sam and
Nicky. Oh what fun you'll have with them! Playing
hide and go seek, and drop the handkerchief, and
baseball; skating and sliding downhill. You'll have
wonderful fun.' And you stared at me and never
winked, as if you were taking it all in and enjoying it.
Then I began to sing to you. I sang lullabies and old
hymns. I remember I sang 'How firm a foundation,
ye saints of the Lord, is laid for your faith in his
excellent Word,' and a lot of other hymns, and you
kept staring at me without winking. And I thought,
'Will this baby *never* go to sleep?' At last your lashes
went slowly down on your cheeks. But then they
flashed open again as if you were afraid you would
miss something. After a little, though, they slowly
went down again. Now and then they would lift a bit
to see if I was still there. But at last your lashes
rested on your cheeks, and I went cautiously over to
the bed and laid you down, with your head on the
pillow, slipping my hand carefully out from under
your head, pulling up the little blue silk quilt, putting
pillows about you so you wouldn't fall off, and you
were asleep!'"

Barry listened radiantly till she had finished and
then he said, "Why, Aunt Faith. I almost remember
that! If I would think a little harder I'm sure I could
remember it clearly. Your face has always reminded
me of something pleasant in my past, and it must
have been that."

As they rose from the table Barry caught Aunt Faith's fingers and squeezed them lovingly.

"Oh, Aunt Faith, I'm so glad you're here!" he said genuinely. "You're so sincere, and you don't *fuss!*"

"Thank you," she said, pressing his fingers affectionately. "That makes me very proud to have you say that!"

They sat for awhile on the porch talking. Barry told her all about the changes on the street.

"See that old house over there on the corner? Do you remember the old ramshackle porch with the pillars all tottering? Well, one day they fell down, and the man had to build a new porch. See those stone arches? Well, I took my stone blocks over there and built a porch with arches for him, and he got the idea and built it. Good work, isn't it? That was the first house I ever 'architected.'

"And see that new house next door to the corner? There's a new bride and groom living there. We don't know them yet, but I don't believe we want to. She's got her face all painted up, and she has plucked eyebrows; her lips are so red they look as if they were bleeding. She's a mess, if you ask me!

"And next door the woman ran away with another man and left her family. He lives at a club, and the children are in boarding schools. The house is closed. It's awful!

"And next door the Millers still live there just as they did. They're kind of drying up. They never go out anywhere.

"And over on this side the Burtons don't do a thing but play bridge and have wild parties. Sometimes you can hear them laugh half the night.

"The house next to them is sold. We don't know yet who bought it. Isn't it painted an awful color? Sort of like pea soup!

"And over here at the left the Parkers still survive, poor as ever and twice as proud! And next to them is Dilly Peterson's cottage. Remember her? Yes, she still lives there, and she's *just* as *disagreeable* as ever!"

He talked on about the other houses up the street, comments for all. Then presently he jumped up, looking at his watch.

"Well, I guess it's time we got started. Will it take you long to get ready?"

"Oh, no. I've just got to get my hat," said Aunt Faith.

So Barry brought his car around and they were soon spinning down the street.

As they drew near to the church Barry was surprised to see so many people going in. He thought he had started very early. And then he was surprised again to see who some of the people were who were entering the church.

"I wonder how they got that old bird!" he said, looking wonderingly at one middle-aged man who was going in. "I never heard he went to church anywhere! He's supposed to be an atheist!"

The church was beginning to fill up when they arrived. Barry led his aunt to the gallery and found a front seat overlooking the audience, not far from a big window where there was a delightful breeze. Down below the people were filing in quickly now, and Aunt Faith was interested in recognizing old acquaintances. Barry kept up a running commentary on them, giving résumés of their history to date, and occasionally amusing comments on their characteristics.

"Quite a mob!" he said, with a kind of sneering wonder in his eyes. It was plain from some of his cryptic sentences that he was amazed to see some of the people who were there. Occasionally he branded one in contempt with the name "hypocrite," but for the most part his remarks were pleasant enough.

Then the organ began to play and the choir filed in. The platform had been extended to accommodate an augmented choir, and in front of the choir seats were two rows of little chairs from the primary room for the children. After the regular choir was seated, from the front door came marching the children led by Joy and another little girl; they looked like sweet little saints in their white dresses and their gold curls. Then came the little boys marching behind. And as they marched they sang:

Wide, wide as the ocean,
  High as the heavens above,
Deep, deep as the deepest sea,
  Is my Savior's love;
And I, though all unworthy
  Still am a child of his care,
For his Word teaches me
  That his love reaches me
Ev'rywhere.

Aunt Faith did not seem to be watching Barry, but her heart was on the alert and she missed not one of the expressions that flitted over his face as he watched his little sister in her white dress, with her bright head lifted and her eager face lighted, marching with the other children down the aisle and filing up to the platform. They sat there looking like so many flowers. The whole incident made a very lovely setting for the meeting that followed.

The leader prayed and Aunt Faith's heart gave thanks. He sounded sincere. She hoped Barry thought so.

Aunt Faith noticed with delight how the singing began to swell and ring out until it almost seemed as if the roof were being lifted. Even Barry seemed to enjoy it, though he did not move his lips to join in it.

When the young evangelist came on the platform Barry studied him keenly, critically. Aunt Faith saw the suggestion of an open mind perhaps, in his glance, but a settled conviction in the set of Barry's lips that this man too was probably a pleasant kind of fake. Still he studied him. And oh, how his aunt prayed that the man who was about to lead the service and give the message might be filled with wisdom from on high!

There followed more singing, enthusiastic, eager, soul-stirring. They sang a number of choruses: "The blood, the blood, is all my plea, Hallelujah, it cleanseth me!" "Calvary covers it all, my past with its sin and shame," and then another which Aunt Faith had never heard before:

I have the love of Jesus, love of Jesus,
  Down in my heart,
Down in my heart, down in my heart,
  I have the love of Jesus, love of Jesus,
Down in my heart,
  Down in my heart to stay.

Barry looked down with an amused sneer on his handsome lips. Aunt Faith's soul shrank away from the sight. It was a sneer of disillusionment, such as an older person might have worn. He was too young to look like that over the enthusiastic singing of a hymn. What could have made him feel that way? Barry, brought up in such a wonderful Christian family!

The audience burst into another verse:

I have the peace that passeth understanding,
  Down in my heart,
Down in my heart, down in my heart,
  I have the peace that passeth understanding,
Down in my heart,
  Down in my heart to stay.

And then Barry snickered right out; almost a snort of mirth, it was. But no, there was more than mere mirth, there was scoffing! Oh, he smothered it quickly behind his hand, but Aunt Faith was startled. What could have happened to Barry to convulse him with mirth about a tender song like that? Did he see something funny in the audience? No, he didn't seem to be looking at anything in particular. Yet again there was that hard, unbelieving look in his eyes.

Barry, her dear boy, Barry!

Then there were prayers. Many prayers, all over the house, most of them brief, only a few sentences, but tender and from the heart.

But Barry didn't even bow his head or close his eyes. He folded his arms and leaned over the railing, identifying each voice as it came, sometimes looking amused, sometimes thoughtful, sometimes sneering again. He didn't even bow his head when his own gray-haired father closed the prayers with a tender petition.

Aunt Faith's heart grew heavy, and she began to pray again for Barry.

They sang one or two more songs and then there were testimonies. All over the house the young people rose and testified, sometimes two or three were standing at once, giving their witness in clear voices.

Barry and Aunt Faith looked down at them, and Aunt Faith's heart thrilled as the testimonies went on.

That was Rosalie down there standing now.

"I want to say that the Lord is dearer to me today than ever before. He is helping me to know what the 'peace that passeth understanding' means."

And Barry suddenly snorted right out.

Oh, he put his hand over his mouth, and tried to clear his throat and convey the idea that he had not laughed, but Aunt Faith, looking furtively at him, saw a fleeting grin on his lips. His pretty sister sat down and several other young people arose to testify. But somehow the aunt got the impression that Barry was not being helped by this part of the meeting, that he seemed to see something behind it all which she could not understand. She found herself wishing that the testimony meeting would be over, for it certainly was not getting across with Barry.

But the testimonies went on. John stood up.

"I am trusting in the blood of Jesus to cover my sins!" he said with a manly ring to his voice, and his brother watching, grinned again. That clear testimony hadn't meant a thing to Barry! Why?

A moment later the twins arose: "I am glad that I have found peace in Jesus," said Jean.

Barry snickered faintly.

"Jesus is all the world to me. I think he is giving me victory over my sins!" said Joan.

Again Barry had difficulty in controlling his laughter, his hard unloving laughter and scorn.

Then over on the other side, away up front, Steve stood up and piped in his clear, boyish treble: "I am not ashamed of the gospel of Christ. For it is the power of God unto salvation!"

Barry frowned and drew a deep, disapproving sigh.

A little later Joy stood up in the front row of the children's choir and said in a soft, sweet voice, "I'm glad Jesus died for me. 'We love him because he first loved us.'"

It was very moving. Aunt Faith found the tears coming into her eyes, but turning suddenly she saw only an annoyed look on the face of the young man beside her. It was as if he were wishing that his family wouldn't say these things. His lips were shut again in that thin line of disapproval. There was no light of either wonder or awe in his eyes.

After that he sat back with his arms folded, and that inscrutable look on his young face. A look that showed as plainly as words could have done that as far as Barry was concerned, the meeting was ended. He had no further interest in what would follow. And in spite of her great desire, and her hope that had grown out of her own prayers, she had a sinking feeling, a certain conviction that nothing now would get across into this young man's heart.

And what was the secret of it? Why should the lovely testimonies of his own dear brothers and sisters, and even the clear ringing testimony of his mother, which came a little later, not move him in the least? She snatched a furtive glimpse at him sitting straight and stern beside her, his arms still folded, his lips still in that grim, set line, and his eyes, his *unbelieving* eyes on the floor.

The sermon that followed was most impressive. At the very first word Aunt Faith knew that Barry's interest was aroused, and that he gave respectful attention to every point. Yet he was like one standing at the top of an amphitheater where an acrobatic entertainment was going on in which he had no personal interest. His mind was assenting to the points made, his sense of humor pleased by several witty stories, his superficial admiration stirred by the personality and magnetism of the speaker, but he himself was miles away from the whole subject that was being discussed, as if it were a thing he had settled long ago as not for him.

Gradually Aunt Faith sensed all this, and knew in some degree what her sister had meant when she sighed and was worried about her eldest boy. And so, quietly, she went on praying. She could not fathom the reason why Barry should be this way. Only the adversary and God knew. Only the Holy Spirit could help here, she was sure, no matter what the cause had been. So she prayed.

At the end of the sermon an invitation was given for all who would accept Christ to come forward, and many came. Barry sat with folded arms leaning over the balcony rail and watched all who went forward, but still with that same sneer on his lips, those same unbelieving eyes. At the very end an old man sitting in the last seat, with the marks of sin on his face, came hesitantly out into the aisle and tottered up to the front. Barry watched him all the way. When he was just opposite where he sat, Barry said in a clear, amused tone: *"Humph!* He won't last long!"

Barry was courteous at the end, greeting old friends, introducing new ones, and they had a pleasant talk.

Then they went out to the car.

"How about a little spin in the moonlight before we go home, Aunt Faith?" Barry asked gaily. "The folks won't be home till all hours. They always stay till the last cat's hung. I'd like to show you the new tennis courts in the park and the fountains and sunken gardens. It's swell out there!"

"Why, yes, I'd enjoy a ride," smiled Aunt Faith.

So they drove about the park and Barry showed her all the changes that had come since she went away. Then he took her a little way out the highway past the new estates. But underneath her apparent interest in what was being said his aunt kept feeling that this was the time, the opportunity that Barry's mother had hoped she would have, yet her lips were dumb. God gave her nothing to say to this dear boy who had wandered away. What was the reason? If those inspiring songs, the testimonies, the prayers, and that wonderful sermon had not reached him, what could she say?

At last they drove back home. When they got to the house they found the children were there ahead of them. They were having an altercation about the radio and their voices were loud and angry.

"I think you're awful mean, Steve! I don't care if you do want to get XYZ. I was here *first*, and I want to hear the Jubilee singers. It's just time for them to begin!" Joy was saying petulantly, and she stamped her small foot furiously at her brother and snatched at his arm.

"Aw, shut up, cantcha!" said the brother. "I want-ta get the time. Cantcha see I'm setting my watch? Look out there! Let that dial alone, you little pest, you!" And suddenly Steve gave Joy a resounding slap on her round pink cheek.

"You horrid mean thing!" screamed Joy, and broke into tempestuous sobs. "I'm going to tell Mother!"

"All right, tell her! And I'll tell Dad! You know

what *he*'ll say. I'm required to set my watch at night or I'll get a bawling out for being late to breakfast! There he comes now. Dad, this kid won't let me get the right time on the radio—!"

"Mother! Steve's spoiling the Jubilee singers and you said I could stay up till they were done singing."

But the father and mother were engaged in an argument and didn't hear them.

"Myra, I tell you you are utterly mistaken. That woman's name is Bartlett, not Brown, and she lives on Second Street."

"It is *not*, it's *Brown!*" declared Myra angrily. "She just told me her name! And the woman with her is her sister. They've just moved here from Buffalo and they're in awful trouble."

"No, her name is Bartlett!" insisted the minister. "I guess I know my own church members! You probably misunderstood her."

"I did *not* misunderstand her! I guess I have as good sense as you have, and I'm not in the least deaf! They've just moved here from Buffalo and her husband is dead."

"Oh no, he isn't dead at all. I tell you I know that woman. She's always in some uncomfortable position and wants help. In fact I called on her the other day and found she'd gone on a picnic. The woman who was with her lives next door to her and she called out to me that she had gone on a picnic."

"John! You are the most exasperating man! It's you who have got things mixed. That woman's name is Brown. She just told me so, and the younger one is her sister, Jane Hawkins, who lives with her. I had a long talk with them before I endeavored to get you to come and speak with them. They wanted to see you and talk with you! They are in great trouble!"

"But, my dear, you saw that I was busy with Mr. Merchant. You must have seen that I was engaged in a most important conversation. I simply couldn't turn away from him to talk with people whom I can see any day. Besides, I'm sure you are mistaken. Those women live down on Second Street!"

"They certainly do not," said the minister's wife, two red spots coming out on her cheeks and making her look in her anger a little like her pretty daughter Rosalie. "You seem to think I have no brains nor ears. Didn't I tell you they told me their names? They said—"

"But my dear, what does it matter what their names are? I tell you I was engaged in a most important conversation. Mr. Merchant was telling me that the minister over in the Second church has been criticizing our methods over here. He says that we are not strictly fundamental, and he's having meetings himself in his own church, beginning next week. He's having that evangelist that talks about himself so much, and *yet* he criticizes *us!* You can see that it was most important that I understand thoroughly the whole matter!"

"*Why*, I should like to know?" snapped his wife. "And what earthly difference does it make what that other minister thinks, anyway? He's not orthodox himself! Besides, John, I think he has put himself in a position where any decent self-respecting man shouldn't even speak to him on the street. Do you know what he told Betty Asher? He told her it was perfectly right for her to get a divorce if she wanted to, *and marry again,* too! And they say that he doesn't approve of foreign missions either! I declare I don't see why you pay the slightest attention to what he says."

"Mother!" howled Joy. "Steve's pulling my hair!"

"I was not, you little pest, you!"

But the mother and father went on arguing and didn't hear.

Barry led Aunt Faith into the library, but the twins were ahead of them, having entered from the pantry where they had been rifling the cake box. They had large pieces of chocolate cake in their hands and were wrangling at the top of their voices.

"I don't see why you can't lend me your new hat to wear tomorrow," said Jean. "You hardly ever wear it, and it's awfully becoming to me. You know I haven't a hat fit to wear to call on those young people at the hotel. They promised to go to church tomorrow night if I came for them. I don't see why you have to be so stingy with your old hat anyway. You are always so terribly mine-and-thine about your things."

"Just because you ruin everything you get, and then come back on me for mine!" said Joan sticking up her chin disagreeably. "You had a new hat at the same time I had mine, and you chose to wear it to the picnic in the rain and get it all out of shape. Now you want to spoil mine! You shan't have mine to slam around!"

"You know that isn't so, Joan Kent! Look at the dress I'm wearing. There isn't a spot on it and yours has had to be cleaned twice, and they were bought at the same time! Besides, what's a hat? It will be all out of fashion before another season. It's an awfully odd shape anyway, and not at all your style. It doesn't become you *in the least!*"

"It does so, it's the most becoming hat I ever had, and if you don't like it why do you want to borrow it? Nothing doing! I'm taking care of my hat, and anyway I hate the idea of people thinking we wear each other's things just because we're twins. Mother, speak to Jean, won't you, and tell her she can't have my hat? She's spoiled her own, and now she wants mine!"

"Mother, won't you tell Joan she's *got* to let me borrow her hat just once? I haven't any hat fit to wear with my new dress to the hotel after those swell New York girls."

But the mother and father were still arguing and didn't hear.

Just then Rosalie and John came in, and Rosalie went straight over to her father and interrupted him, laying her hand on his arm.

"Dad, what do you think?" she said, her eyes very bright and her cheeks as pink as if they had been painted. "Mrs. Cromwell, the lady who lives in that big new estate up the highway, was in the meeting tonight, and she heard me sing that solo in the anthem, and liked it so much she's asked me to sing at her garden party next month! Isn't that perfectly wonderful!"

"Aw, *you!* You think you have a *voice!*" sneered her brother John. "You hit at least three sour notes tonight!"

"Sez *you!*" flashed Rosalie, lifting her chin, anger snapping in her eyes. "What do *you* know about music? You think because you can strum on the guitar that you can criticize everybody! You can't tell a sour note from a sweet one. I can tell you I get mighty sick of your everlasting strumming on those old twangy strings. Keeping us awake at night and waking us up in the morning. What in the world you ever took up that instrument for, I don't see. It's no earthly good to anybody! Just so you can sit there by the hour and roll your eyes and sing silly love songs. If you'd get a real instrument and take lessons you might someday be in a position to tell a sour note from a sweet one, but at present your opinion isn't worth much."

"Well, I wasn't the only one who thought so," said John with a superior smile. "That Mr. Grant and his simpering wife were laughing at you. They've studied at some conservatory or other, and every time you sang that high G or C or whatever you call it, your voice went sour, and they laughed! All righty! You can turn up your nose, and you can go right on singing in public and making a fool of yourself if you want to, singing *sour* notes if you don't know the difference. But don't flatter yourself people enjoy it! That Mrs. Cromwell is no musician if she thought you sang beautifully. *Not me!* You just spoiled the whole service for me! *My sister* singing *sour notes!* I wished the floor would open and let me through. I was *ashamed* of you, and *that's the truth!*"

"Oh, *shut up!*" said Rosalie in a loud angry voice.

And then came a wild hysterical sob from little Joy on the stairs:

"Mother! Steve *is* pulling my hair!"

"I wasn't pulling your hair!" snarled Steve, coming down the steps with an angry thump.

Suddenly Barry, who had come back into the hall and was standing in the doorway, began to sing in a high, sweet tenor:

I have the peace that passeth understanding,
  Down in my heart,
Down in my heart, down in my heart,
  I have the peace that passeth understanding,
Down in my heart,
  Down in my heart to stay!

He sang it all the way through amid an awful silence! Everyone in the room knew exactly what he meant. Even little Joy up there on the stairs, with two great tears rolling down her round pink cheeks, and two more just ready to follow, and her mouth open for another howl, stopped short and stared at him. Little Joy had been praying for Barry, and now she suddenly saw how she had been undoing her prayers by her actions here at home.

They all knew.

It was as if the words they had just been speaking were up there in the top of the room pointing down at them, accusing, condemning them. They could almost hear the echo of their angry voices lingering on the air. They listened to Barry with startled, horrified eyes, their faces growing white and shamed. They looked at the merry, worldly face of their brother as he sang and were condemned. They knew the witness of their lives before this unbelieving brother had belied the words they had spoken from their eager hearts in church.

The mother stood aghast, incredulous. Could it be that such little everyday homely contacts as this had led Barry away from God?

Steve, as he stood behind the big overstuffed chair, understood, and the words of the song went deep into his heart. He could still hear his own raucous voice calling his little sister names. Slowly his lashes drooped as the song went on, his gaze went down, his head bowed, he sank down lower and lower out of sight, till he was sitting on the floor with his face against the plush of the chair.

It was as if all around that room there was a panorama of the acts and words of that family, especially during the last few weeks while the evangelist had been with them, and they had all been working to save souls!

John, standing in front of the big back window, suddenly and silently turned himself about, and catching the heavy crimson curtains one in each hand, he brought them quietly together behind his back, obliterating himself; he stood there gazing into the darkness of the backyard seeing himself as God must see him, for the first time in his life.

The twins had giggled when Barry first began to sing, then they looked at each other with shamed glances, their eyes fell, and they silently turned and slowly melted out of the room into the dark dining room.

Rosalie blanched and stared at Barry wide-eyed. For underneath all her silliness and foolish pride and conceit, Rosalie was real, and she truly wanted Barry to come back to God. She had been earnestly praying for him every day. And now she saw how her own words and actions had led him astray, and her heart was filled with deep remorse and sorrow.

But it was the gray-haired father most of all who winced at that song. He had given his life to the service of God and longed more than anything else to be able to lead people to the Lord Jesus Christ, and now he saw how in the little daily contacts of life he had been leading his beloved eldest son away from Christ.

He had come to stand by the mantel, with his elbow on the shelf and his head bowed on his hand, while that song was going on, and when it was finished he lifted his head and looked at Barry.

"That's the way we've looked to you, Barry! That's the way we've been!" he said in a tone of deep sorrow.

"Oh, *Dad!*" said Barry, suddenly apologetic, "I was only *kidding!*"

"Yes, but it was true!" said the father. "That's the way we've been. That's what we have done! And you've made us see ourselves!"

And then as if the Lord had suddenly come into the room, the gray-haired father turned and began to talk to God.

"Oh, Lord," he said slowly, his hands clasped before him as he looked up, while the family stood petrified and listened. "Oh, Lord, *I've sinned!* We've *all* sinned! But *I* most of all. And now I'm glad you've sent me word about it. Lord, I didn't know I was doing that! But now, Lord, I can't do anything about it myself. It's an awful habit that I didn't realize, and by myself I can't cure it. But—I'm handing over my sinful self to you now, to be put to death daily. Do it *now*, Lord, at *any cost*, and live the life of my Lord in me, that others may see thee and not myself in me!"

With broken heart, the gray-haired father went down upon his knees beside the big chair to pray half the night.

And one by one the family stole shamedly up the stairs to their rooms, to meet their conscience and their God. Till only Barry was left, standing in the doorway, looking with misty eyes at his father, listening as his father confessed his sins aloud to God!

"*Dad!*" he said in a husky, choking voice, "it was only a *joke!* I didn't mean a thing!"

But his father was talking aloud to God and didn't hear.

"Dad! *Oh, Dad!*"

Then suddenly Barry turned, brushing away a quick tear, and with a last lingering look at his father kneeling there, he strode up the stairs to his room, to meet *his* conscience and *his* God!

And up in the guest room Aunt Faith was kneeling by her bed, thanking God that the Holy Spirit has ways of working that mortals may not use.

THE OLD
GUARD

MRS. Dunlap, Mrs. Bryan, and Miss Dewy arrived at the church fifteen minutes before the appointed hour for the missionary meeting. It was their custom to do so.

Until a few months ago there had been four of them, but God had called the fourth one, Mrs. Bonner, first to be laid low on a bed of sickness and then, just six weeks ago, to go home to him. Mrs. Bonner had been their leader, and for many years the president of their society. She had been a slim, sweet, fair little woman with a consecrated mind, body, and fortune, and gifted with the power of leadership to an extraordinary degree.

Even while she lay sweetly, uncomplainingly upon her bed, in what they all knew was her last illness, the power of her consecrated life had gone out almost as when she walked among them. Her Christianity was vital and held them like a magnet. Even the worldly church members acknowledged her gentle but firm leadership and followed where she led, at least from afar.

Miss Dewy was short and sharp-tongued, keen, quick-tempered, and sarcastic, but she loved her Lord devotedly. She shed many tears and spent many hours of earnest prayer over her own short-comings, but she had been known to tell a fellow member exactly how she thought that member looked to the eyes of God, offending her beyond reparation, and then to agonize in prayer for her all night long.

Mrs. Bryan was a meek, quiet little creature with prematurely gray hair and chastened eyes, but a faith in God and a power in prayer that stopped at nothing. She had seen much sorrow in her life but had let it bring forth the fruit of righteousness. She wore plain clothes and gave astonishingly to missions. People ignored her except when there was hard work to be done, and then they hunted her up and said it was "so good of her to be willing." Somehow she could always find time to visit the poor and the sick, and could usually produce many partly worn garments for people who needed them.

Mrs. Dunlap was a hard-working woman with a crippled son to support and a way of leaning hard upon God. She had seen better days and was well educated, having acquired a deep culture which her hard work had not eradicated.

All three of these women believed with all their hearts in prayer.

They had met often with Mrs. Bonner, even during her last illness, to pray for their beloved church and missionary society. And now, even since Mrs. Bonner was gone, they carried on. They came early to the meetings to pray. They had no other convenient place to meet.

The women in the church who knew about it thought it strange of them. They felt somehow rebuked when they came upon them in prayer. "Just without any reason at all!" they said in vexed tones, backing out of the vestibule to wait till the devotions were over. "*Just* to *pray!* How odd of them!" They called them "The Old Guard" and laughed a little derisively. Presently the name got around among the women of the church, "The Old Guard!"

The Old Guard entered the dim quiet of the ladies' parlor and went straight to the sacred corner where they had brought so many perplexing problems in the past to the Throne of Grace, and prayed them through. There they knelt in their accustomed corner and began to talk to God. Their hearts were heavily burdened for their dear society, yet there was a ring of triumph and thanksgiving to their opening words. They had to thank God first for the way everything had worked out, for just the night before, the session of the church had formally approved the appointing of Mary Lee to go to India as their own special missionary.

Of course it had been rather expected for the last three years while Mary Lee, under the patronage of Mrs. Bonner, had been completing her course at Bible school with that in mind. But now that Mrs. Bonner was gone, the Old Guard had greatly feared that the church might lose interest in that project which had been so dear to Mrs. Bonner's heart.

Therefore, thanksgiving about Mary Lee had been first on their lips in the prayers they uttered. And after that, less jubilantly, there was tender prayer for the new president of the society, Mrs. Lansing Searle. She was to take charge that day for the first time, and in proportion as these good women feared for her ability to take the place of the sainted Mrs. Bonner, so they waited on the Lord in prayer that he might endue her with wisdom from above. It was not their votes that had made Mrs. Searle president; but the majority of the members were intrigued by having a woman of such wealth and social prominence among them, and the Old Guard had been outvoted.

Mrs. Lansing Searle was pretty and popular. She had honey-colored hair, most appealing eyes, a firm little red mouth, and wore orchid costumes. The name wasn't hyphenated, but her friends always spoke it as if it were, rhythmically, Mrs. *Lansing*-Searle, as if any other Searle were not worth mentioning. She was small and gentle-looking, and one couldn't imagine that she would be anything but a figurehead. But she had an amazingly stubborn chin, and tight little lips that could sneer. Mrs. Dunlap's crippled son, who had uncanny insight into character even from his invalid chair by the street window, said she was the devil's best counterfeit of a saint. Of course, Chester Dunlap himself was not yet sanctified in his own life. But so, all the more Chester Dunlap's mother laid the new missionary society president in the care of the Almighty and pled for

her soul. It is to be hoped that Mrs. Lansing Searle
would not have laughed had she heard that prayer.
For the Old Guard had laid aside their prejudices and
their preconceived fears, and were praying as if their
very life, and the life of the missionary society, de-
pended upon it—as perhaps it did.

The three dear souls had got so far into communion with the other world as to have lost their fears
and dropped their burdens again and had gone back
to climax their prayers with another little paean of
joy about Mary Lee and India, when Mrs. Appleby
and a flock of followers arrived unaccustomedly in
the vestibule and paused an instant to look around.
Mrs. Appleby was the new vice-president. She was
large and well-groomed, with a baby complexion,
perfect teeth, and big fat pearls in her ears. Her
costume reminded one of a flourishing apple tree in
blossom, green with a touch of rose about her hat,
exceedingly smart. Jerome Appleby, her husband,
was a great clubman.

"Let's see, girls, which door goes into the Ladies'
Parlor? This one? I declare I don't know my way
around here!" she babbled, and then with her followers boomed into the quiet hush where prayer per-
vaded the atmosphere.

"My soul! Is there something going on here already? We can't be late!" she blustered noisily.

"Sh! There's someone praying!" whispered Mrs.
Melton, who was always afraid of doing the wrong
thing.

"It's only the Old Guard," giggled young Mrs.
Stacey in an ill-suppressed whisper. "My word!

Wouldn't you think they'd have the politeness to wait till the new president arrives to open the meeting?"

The soft voice of prayer in the corner dropped into a quiet amen, and the three devoted women arose and took their seats, not even looking the indignation that mortal Christian women could scarce help feeling.

The huddled invaders of the holy place stood uncertainly by the door conversing in subdued tones, a trifle awed, perhaps even a little shamed by the dignity of those three quiet backs. A moment later Mrs. Lansing Searle entered gaily with a trilling laugh to her companion. She gave a quick searching glance around, taking in the Old Guard without seeming to do so, and then, assuming a gentle attitude of superiority, went forward to the desk and took her place with much self-possession—just as though she had always been president of that society; just as though this was not the very first time she had ever had anything to do with a missionary society.

Of course she was a clubwoman. She had a reputation for being one of the best parliamentarians in town. She could recite Roberts' Rules of Order from start to finish, and she could make a charming and graceful speech. These had been qualifications for the position intensively urged at her election.

After she had arranged her notebook and a few papers she had brought with her on the desk, and glanced at her trinket of a wristwatch, she signaled to the piano one of the frivolous young women who had arrived in her company, and who, obviously, was not a frequenter of missionary meetings. Then she looked around with a smile.

"Ladies, will you please come to order?" she said, although there was not the slightest sign of disorder in the room.

The group around Mrs. Appleby came about-face and selected seats in the shadows near the rear.

"Let us open the meeting by singing number two seventy-three," announced the president in a clear voice after having consulted the bit of paper on the desk.

Now Mrs. Lansing Searle was not familiar with hymnology, neither did her home contain any very great selection of hymnbooks, but the women who had so earnestly engineered her election to the office of president because they wished to secure her influence and social standing for their church, had carefully supplied her with one of the church hymnals and it had reposed on top of the piano in her home all week. At the very last minute while she was powdering her nose and putting on her scrap of a hat, she had remembered it and called to her young daughter Edwina.

"Darling, won't you run down and pick me out a couple of hymns for that meeting I'm to lead this afternoon? I forgot all about it. Get good old ones that everybody knows."

So Edwina had carefully selected "Nearer, My God, to Thee" and "Onward Christian Soldiers" and written their numbers into her mother's neat program.

But the janitor had unfortunately forgotten to gather up the hymnbooks from the Christian Endeavor rally held the night before, in order to distribute the church hymnals which the missionary society always used. So it was not the good old staid hymnbook that the ladies reached for, fluttering the leaves to find number two seventy-three, but a cheery little gospel songbook.

However, the majority of ladies present were utterly new to the ways of this missionary society, and willingly began to sing the rousing old song, "Hold the Fort." Even Mrs. Searle was none the wiser, for she had left her own book at home on the piano, and so quite cheerfully entered into the song:

Ho my comrades, see the signal waving in the sky!
Reinforcements now appearing, Victory is nigh.

The new president sang her satisfaction in the selection and thought how keen her Edwina was to select so appropriate a song, although the tune did seem a bit odd. But, reinforcements! Who, but herself and the bright new friends she had brought into this dull old society to give it new life, were the reinforcements? She let out her cultured voice in full power on "Hold the fort for I am coming!" and "waved the answer back to heaven" with great gusto: "By thy grace *we will!*" without a thought of him by whose grace alone they could possibly hope to win. She was only exulting in what an appropriate selection Edwina had found.

But by the time the second verse was reached, her attention was called to the outer door, which

swung back just as Mrs. Cresswell Kingdon entered
in all the glory of a new black satin spring costume.
She wore long jet earrings dangling on her shoulders, and her sharp, haughty face was flushed with
brick-colored rouge, in a sort of permanent flush.
She was followed by nine other smartly attired
women. Here at last was the important contingent!
Mrs. Searle had been afraid they were going to fail
her after all.

The room was fairly filled with quiet elderly
women now, the regular old members of the missionary society scattered here and there among the people who were to give new life to them, looking a bit
like barnyard fowls among the peacocks. But when
Mrs. Cresswell Kingdon entered with her friends, a
little stir of surprise and something almost like fear
entered the old ranks of faithful ones.

They came in noisily, breezily, almost as if they
were amused at themselves for being there, but Mrs.
Searle smiled complacently and opened her voice to
sing its best as they advanced toward the front
seats.

"See the mighty host advancing!" sang the ladies
earnestly, "Satan leading on!"

Mrs. Dunlap looked up suddenly and saw Mrs.
Cresswell Kingdon leading her troop of society ladies
and suddenly put down her head and put up her
handkerchief to cover a smile. She lived in too close
touch with her irreverent, fun-loving son not to see
the humorous side of things. But nobody else saw it,
and least of all the new president who was still re-
flecting on Edwina's perspicacity.

When the song was ended Mrs. Lansing Searle readjusted her papers, and with as much self-possession as she had ever used in presiding over a club meeting, she said:

"Let us pray!"

She selected obviously the second of the papers that lay on her desk, spread it before her, and without any attempt to close her eyes she read her prayer in a pleasant conversational tone.

"Lord, we thank thee today that there are so many gifted people here who are willing to devote their time and their talents and their ability to building up thy kingdom. We feel sure that thou wilt bless our plans for making the world better, and wilt bring great good out of this little meeting today. We know that a little leaven leaveneth the whole lump, and so our efforts here, though begun in a small way, will presently increase and cover the whole earth, and thy kingdom shall at length come on earth through our efforts. Amen."

Mrs. Dunlap heard Persis Dewy draw her breath in a quick little breath of protest at the word about leaven being compared to good. She began to pray softly that Persis would not feel that she must jump right up after the prayer and enlighten the new president, telling her that leaven always stood for evil in the Bible, never for good. It would be like Persis to do that in her eagerness to instruct everybody in the dispensational truth in which she was so much interested.

But the new president gave Persis Dewy no time

to spoil her Christian testimony with her sarcastic little tongue. The devotional ceremony being thus glibly disposed of by a hymn and a prayer, she hastened on to the business of the hour.

"Ladies," she said sweetly, "I want to thank you for the honor you have done me in making me your president, and I intend to take this office over conscientiously and do my very best for you. I have been informed that the society has been somewhat vegetating during the illness of our dear Mrs. Bonner, for naturally while she was laid aside she was not able to keep up with the times. We must not blame her for that. She did her best, I am sure, and we are all so glad that she is free from pain and has passed to her reward.

"But now, ladies, I am sure you all feel with me that we must get to work promptly and bring things up to date. And to that end I have invited in some new members who will be glad to help us reconstruct things. I have talked over plans with some of them and find them quite willing to work, and they really have some charming ideas. I know you will be delighted with them when you hear them. But now the first thing is to get these people signed up so that they can help us vote on all the questions that come up. Mrs. Archer, our new secretary, unfortunately could not be present today as she had a previous engagement, so I will appoint Miss Dewy, the former secretary, to be secretary pro tem. Miss Dewy, will you just take the names of the new members? Mrs. Appleby, you are our new treasurer, will you

kindly follow Miss Dewy around and take the dues?
A dollar and a half each, isn't it? Yes, I thought I
was right."

Persis Dewy, grim and wrathy, arose with her roll
book and started out among the elite, grudgingly
allowing them to write their names under the beloved names of saintly members of the past. It
seemed to her a desecration. But one could not refuse to accept new members to a missionary society.
And nearly all those present were members of the
church. What could she do? She resented the fact
that these rich, worldly women were being brought
into the society to bolster up the funds of the organization. She very much doubted the wisdom of
raising money by any such strategy. She did not feel
that the Lord would be pleased with money acquired
in this way. But she had just been praying with the
Old Guard that the Lord might have his way in her,
and she knew that the Lord would not let one of his
own plans be frustrated, so she went about with her
book and held her peace.

There was a little stir in the meeting, some
laughing and talking among the new people, a bit of
banter among the younger ones. The old members
looked about a trifle worried. It did not seem like the
usual atmosphere of their precious meeting which
they had always so enjoyed in Mrs. Bonner's day.
But it was soon over, and Mrs. Lansing Searle sailed
into the preliminaries of the business of the day,
showing great skill and prowess, as well as an intimate knowledge of the details of the society that had
been placed under her control. The quiet, meek

members who had heretofore gone with fear and trembling through the intricacies of motions and secondings, and had taken their votings seriously with due consideration, now found themselves so hustled from one point to another that they were almost mentally out of breath. They presently arrived at the crux of the matter, the real reason for this meeting, which was Mary Lee and the matter of arranging for her support as the church's own special missionary in India.

The president glided smoothly from the old business to the matter of deepest interest to them all, saying that they had come together to consider the matter of sending a special missionary from the church to some foreign point to "elevate and uplift humanity," but she said not one word about Mary Lee. And it was almost time for Mary Lee to arrive! Could it be possible that Mrs. Lansing Searle had not been informed that she was coming to speak to them?

At last Mrs. Dunlap arose, taking advantage of the president's brief pause for breath, and dared to interrupt.

"Madam President," she said, and her cultured voice drew instant attention, even from the new members whom the president had commandeered. It had always been a source of annoyance to Mrs. Lansing Searle whenever she had given enough attention to the woman to think about her at all, that Mrs. Dunlap should possess such a cultured voice in spite of her shabby clothes.

"Madam President, pardon me for interrupting,"

went on the cultured voice, "but I wasn't sure whether anyone had told you that we are to have the pleasure of a few words from our missionary, Miss Mary Lee herself, this afternoon. I thought I would mention it before she comes in. She is due to arrive almost any minute now and will have to talk as soon as she comes because she has only a brief time and must hurry away."

"Oh *really?*" said Mrs. Searle with a lifting of her eyebrows and a quality in her tone that small boys use when they say, "Oh *yeah?*" "But my dear Mrs. Dunlap, that won't be necessary at this time. We might have the janitor telephone her not to come if you know the address. We really haven't time for anything like that this afternoon. We have important business to transact and these ladies," with a swift glance toward the smart group of newcomers, "have given us their important time to come and help us. They are very busy women, you know, and have engagements every hour in the day."

Mrs. Searle smiled as if that settled the question.

But Mrs. Dunlap, with the sternness of a prophet of old, held her ground.

"You don't understand, Mrs. Searle. This has all been arranged for. Mrs. Bonner herself saw to it before she died that Mary Lee should have permission to get away from her afternoon class in the Bible school where examinations are now going on for the end of the term. It was to have been Mrs. Bonner's surprise for her beloved society, and she took great pleasure in feeling that though she could not be here herself she could have a little part in planning this meeting. And—" as the vestibule door swung wide letting in a young girl with sweet eyes and a quiet manner, "here comes Mary Lee now! She can take only a very few minutes, and she was promised that she could speak at once. Come right up front, Mary Lee! We know you haven't much time to spare, and we're just so glad to see you and have a few words from our very own missionary. Ladies, this is Mary Lee, who is going out to India shortly to preach the gospel for us."

Oh, Mrs. Dunlap knew very well she was being officious, but what else could she do? As she sat down and Mary Lee came smiling to the front there was a feeble applause from the old quiet members of the society, ending in a painful questioning sound, as if perhaps they had not done the right thing.

The new contingent simply sat and stared at this plainly dressed, flower-faced girl who stepped to the front, gave a lovely smile to the haughty president, and began to speak at once:

"Dear friends, I am so glad to have this chance to thank you all for giving me the opportunity to go and tell the story of salvation to a people who have never heard of Jesus Christ their Savior.

"It was five years ago that I discovered Jesus Christ to be *my* Savior. I was brought up, as you know, in a Christian home. I went to church and Sunday school. I even taught a Sunday school class, but I was not a Christian myself until five years ago. I was not saved! I did not think I needed to be saved. I thought I was quite good enough for God's standards.

"As I look back on that time I see now that I was in just the same situation as the people in India to whom I am going. So many of them do not feel the need of a Savior from *sin*.

"But God had to show me that I was utterly sinful through and through according to his standards. It was a bitter knowledge that I had to learn, that I was not one whit better in any way or more fit to stand before him than any so-called heathen. It was when I saw myself like that, as a sinner, that I cried out to God and he showed me Jesus Christ as my Savior. I saw my Lord hanging there on the cross for me. I knew it was my sins that had nailed him there. And ever since then I have wanted to take to others the glad news that there is a Savior who has taken away the sin of the world, a Savior who is able to *keep* those that put their trust in him.

"I tell you this today so that you may know why I am going out to the far field in India. And I know that I am not going uselessly nor foolishly, for the Savior that I take to them is able to save souls and 'there is none other name under heaven given among men whereby we must be saved.'

"It is a delight to me to look into your faces this afternoon. I shall remember you all when I am far away and it will be sweet to know that you are praying for me and loving the work as much as I. Because, you know, it is *your* work. Through sending me out there you yourselves are really leading those people for whom Jesus died, to know him, 'whom to know is life eternal.'

"I thank you all for letting me say these few words

to you and I hope I'll know you better before I actually go." Her eyes rested fleetingly, almost questioningly, upon Mrs. Cresswell Kingdon, who sat frowning in amazed disapproval behind her brick-red rouge. "Now I'm sure you will excuse me, for I must hurry right back to my class."

Mary Lee smiled shyly and went swiftly down the aisle and out the door amid an awkward silence that lasted till the door had swung behind her.

It wasn't the kind of reception that Mrs. Bonner had planned for the girl who was so dear to her heart and whom she had been helping to fit for her great work abroad. The hearts of the Old Guard were boiling with shame and indignation, but there wasn't a thing they could have done about it. It was Mrs. Searle's place to give this girl a few words of welcome at the very least. But no, they had let her walk away, and though she was just modest Mary Lee and thought very little of herself, she could not help but sense the coldness in that meeting.

Mrs. Bryan wiped away a few futile tears, Mrs. Dunlap sat sternly fixing the new president with an anguished eye of reproof, and Miss Dewy's little earnest face simply boiled with righteous rage. But the new president was utterly oblivious. She stood haughtily in her orchid robes like an offended princess, and then smiled a slow, amused, contemptuous smile toward her own friends.

"Well, really! Quite an unexpected innovation!" She laughed lightly and murmured: "Oh, well, not *much* time lost!" with a glance at her watch.

The Old Guard sat unsmiling, with downcast eyes,

trying to pray, trembling in their souls. The rest of
the former members didn't quite know what it was
all about, but sensed a hostile attitude, sat timidly
on the fence, so to speak, and waited to see what the
outcome would be.

"Now, ladies, to return to essentials," laughed the
president, tapping lightly with a gold pencil on the
desk, "you will please come to order. I believe we
are ready for business again. And before we go any
further I am going to ask one of our new members
to tell us something of a plan she has been hearing
about. It will, I think, give us an entirely new vision
of what missionary work should be, and create new
impetus to work for it. I have some delightful plans
which I shall unfold to you when you have heard
Mrs. Kingdon speak. Mrs. Kingdon has recently
attended a large mass meeting in New York where
the ideas she has to offer were brought forward, and
from all I hear it is the beginning of a new era in
church missions. Mrs. Kingdon, will you tell us all
that you have told me?"

Then up rose Mrs. Kingdon, the permanent flush
on her cheeks, and the dangling glitter of her earrings somehow out of keeping with all ideas of a
missionary meeting. But Mrs. Kingdon did not seem
at all embarrassed to be addressing such a body. She
arose briskly with an air of knowing about everything, and began to speak.

"Ladies, this is the first time I have ever been in
a missionary meeting in my life! Missions have never
appealed to me before. But I have been glad to learn
recently that missions as a whole have taken a new

turn, new methods are entering in, new standards being raised, and I have come to feel that missions under the new conditions can be made quite worthwhile.

"I do not know whether or not you are all aware that there have been recent investigations into mission work abroad. Some startling facts have been brought to light which have made a few brave souls who have done the investigating speak their minds. And there has not been lacking an eager response by many thinking women of today, who under the former regime held aloof from the efforts that were being put forth in a narrow and bigoted way to force dogmas upon a people who already had their own religion and resented having a new one forced upon them.

"We have no right to try to force our views upon others nor to say that there is but one way of salvation, whatever that term salvation may mean. I'm sure *I* don't know. We must look upon other nations as merely brothers in a common quest for truth and beauty and righteousness. Because some of us happen to believe in Jesus in our land is no reason why we should discount Buddha or Mohammed. We should learn to be tolerant, to live out the spirit of Jesus who went about doing good. We cannot do good to people whom we antagonize by trying to force some traditional dogmas and beliefs upon them. They have a right to their own religion. There is great danger, in the present mode of carrying on foreign mission work, of subordinating the educational to the religious objective. For that reason it is most important whom we send to the foreign field to represent us.

"You will pardon the personal reference, but it seems to me that we have had an illustration brought before us, in the words of the young girl who just attempted to make a speech. Such cant as that is most unfortunate! It is a specimen of what I have been talking about—theological dogma as an obsession. What possible good could such talk do the heathen? What they need is practical uplift! They need to be taught how to grow better crops, to have better homes, to understand and appreciate the beauties in life.

"With all due respect to dear Mrs. Bonner—and no one appreciates more than I all that she has done and sacrificed of her time and money and herself— yet she was behind the time! She was shut away so long by illness that she did not realize that the world had moved on beyond a mere fanatical belief in a tradition that no one who is at all up with the times could possibly accept. It seems to me, Madam President, that it would be most unfortunate in more ways than one if a girl like the one to whom we have just listened should be sent forth to represent our church. Narrow, ignorant, fanatical, and absolutely untrained, ranting of outgrown formulas! We are done with such things in this age of intelligence. Evangelism is no longer the way to reach the masses! The world wants practical help! It appeals for an eternal gospel emancipated from unalterable dogmas built around absurd theological doctrines, many of them long disproved; stereotyped patterns of doctrine and static phrases which have gone dead!"

The high-sounding phrases slipped from the thin, hard Kingdon lips with authority, almost with arrogance, and the gathering of zealous women, almost overpowered by the new voices that had so astonishingly joined their ranks, sat bewildered and blinked at this strange new teaching. Only the Old Guard really understood the full purport of the remarks and sat aghast, driven to quick silent prayer as the speaker swept on her devastating way.

"We are done with oral evangelism, the kind of missionary work which this Miss Lee, to whom we have been listening, evidently represents. Human service without any words at all is better than evangelism. Medical missions represent in themselves the essentials of the Christian enterprise. We need to help make people well and strong and to teach them how to plant their farms to advantage. Planting corn and potatoes in the best way is far more important than working on their emotions to make them believe something that only a small percentage of the world really accepts anymore."

Mrs. Dunlap was listening intently now, her kindly face flushed with excitement, her heart praying, "Oh God, teach us what to do, what to say, how to keep still, and to speak only at the right moment."

"And now," said Mrs. Cresswell Kingdon, "I want to say, before I introduce my helpers who are willing to go to work at once on this campaign of raising the money for the enterprise in hand, that I feel we should utterly put out of our minds any idea of sending out this untaught girl to whom we have just been listening. And I am not offering wholly destructive criticism. I have a lovely substitute in mind. She is a graduate of one of our great modern universities, holds a diploma from a well-known medical college, has had a full nurse's training, and has taken a two years' course in agriculture, as well as various minor cultural courses which would be of untold value in a foreign land. She is also an accomplished linguist and would easily acquire the language wherever she went. She has in addition a charming personality, being young and quite good looking. And it just happens that it would be possible for us to get her services because she has planned to spend at least four or five years in the Orient pursuing some research work for her university, and she could just as well do our work *on the side!* I felt we were in great luck when I heard it, and I went to her at once and secured an option on her services for our church. She has had several other openings brought to her attention, but she has promised to wait one week before she considers the others. Her mother is a very dear friend of mine and that, of course, is why we have the preference. Now, ladies, I simply want your ratification of this and I can secure her at once."

Suddenly Mrs. Ryder, a quiet, meek woman in an old-fashioned brown hat and a shabby suit arose in the row of seats across the aisle from the elegant Mrs. Kingdon and, facing toward her, said in a trembly voice, frightened half out of her timid senses: "Excuse me for interrupting, but *is she a Christian?*"

Mrs. Kingdon turned her brick-colored scorn upon

the woman and fairly withered her with a glance. Then she looked to the president for protection, this interruption being out of order, and met that small dignitary's amused smile. She echoed a smile on her own face that said: "Of course this woman doesn't know any better and it isn't worthwhile to flaunt parliamentary rules at her." Then she brought her glance back to the frightened questioner who was still standing, holding her own.

Mrs. Kingdon, with a contemptuous smile, stared at the interrupter from the toe of her shabby shoe to the crown of her antiquated hat and answered:

"I'm sure I don't know, my dear. We don't go around asking people personal questions like that, do we? But I suppose of course she is, since she knows the request comes from a church. She isn't a heathen, at any rate," and Mrs. Kingdon turned back to her waiting audience as if the matter were ended.

The subdued questioner slumped quickly into her seat with a troubled look in her eyes and subsided. Mrs. Kingdon went rapidly on to the finish.

"So, just to bring this matter to a quick conclusion," she said disagreeably, "I'll make the motion, Madam President, that we approve the appointment of Miss Ann Patricia Melville as our special missionary from our church."

But before she had time to sit down, and before the president could arrange her complacent little mouth to put the question, Mrs. Dunlap arose with dignity and, looking toward the desk, said: "Madam President, may I ask whether Mrs. Kingdon and the rest of the meeting know that the session have already appointed Miss Mary Lee as our missionary, at a special meeting held for that purpose last evening?"

There was a little stir in the room, especially among the old members, a lifting of brows, a look of relief on some faces, a nod here and there, a quick disapproving glance toward the strangers in the room, and then every eye was fastened on Mrs. Kingdon, who had turned her cold stare on Mrs. Dunlap.

But Mrs. Dunlap did not belong to the Old Guard for nothing. She was not afraid to look the elegant Mrs. Kingdon in the eye as calmly as that lady herself could look. So after an instant Mrs. Kingdon's look melted into amusement. She shrugged her shoulders slightly and smiled toward Mrs. Searle.

"I fancy that it won't be hard to convince the session that they have made a mistake and need to rescind that action," she said calmly. "I'll be willing to undertake that personally. And now, ladies," she went on, ignoring Mrs. Dunlap, who was still standing and who by right had the floor, "suppose we go on and explain our plans a little farther before I put that motion. And to that end I want to introduce Mrs. Phil Wentworth. She has some delightful ideas which I'm sure you will enjoy."

Young Mrs. Wentworth arose with vivacity and, being immediately recognized by the chair, proceeded to unfold her plans.

"We have a perfectly thrilling play we are going to put on!" she said engagingly. "We've worked it all out, assigned the characters and everything, and we're going to be ready to produce it by the middle or last of next month. We're planning to sell tickets at a good price which will cover the full cost of production and net us at least a third of the sum required to carry out Mrs. Kingdon's plans. We shall expect every member of the society to be responsible for the sale of at least ten tickets, either selling them or paying for them herself. We have a very wonderful item to announce right at the start; we have secured the services of a professional trainer to get our play in shape, and a real live star herself to take the principal part in the play, so you can be assured that it will be a great success. It's a real thriller! I'm not going to tell you any more just now, but I'm sure that's enough to make you all wildly enthusiastic about selling the tickets!"

The young woman sat down amid a joyous patter of gloved hands and many smiles from the new contingent.

"And now let me introduce Mrs. Lola Duane," said Mrs. Kingdon quickly, before anyone else had a chance to interrupt. "She is the second of my delightful surprises."

Mrs. Lola Duane seemed a child barely out of high school. But in reality she was a youthful divorcee, daughter of a wealthy member of the church. She arose dimpling and lifting her long, effective lashes.

"And *I* am going to give a dance and bridge party combined," said Mrs. Duane, giving the meeting a glance that took them all into her confidence. "Isn't that going to be perfectly *darling?* I'm giving it at one of the large hotels so that we can have all the room we need. It's to be a costume dance for the young people, and a bridge party for the older ones. I'll tell you some of the unique features a little later when I have had time to get them all thought out perfectly. But *I* am going to be responsible for the *second* third of the money to send Miss Ann Patricia Melville to India, and we shall expect you all to be interested and try to further our plans, of course. It will be a subscription dance, and even if you can't come you can all buy tickets."

Mrs. Duane sat down amid more glove clapping and Mrs. Kingdon introduced her third assistant, Miss Charlotte Thayer, a well-tailored, perfectly groomed woman in her early forties.

"And *I* am going to give a progressive dinner!" said Miss Thayer in a throaty voice. "I have secured the loan of a large number of the handsomest homes in the city for our use on the evening selected, and we will have the fruit cup course at one house, the soup at another, the meat course at another, the salad at another, and the dessert at another. Some of these homes are the showplaces of the city and it will be a rare opportunity for those who have not the social entré into such homes to see the beautiful works of art which their more favored fellow citizens have gathered about them. We are charging enough for the tickets to cover taxi fare from one house to another. There will be minor details to be arranged later, but I am sure I have told you enough to make you exceedingly enthusiastic about rooting for this dinner. And *I* am going to be responsible for the *last* third of the money to send Miss Ann Patricia Melville to India!"

There arose quite a clamor of delight among the new members as Miss Thayer sat down, and for a moment the room was in a hubbub. Then the president tapped on her table for quiet.

"Ladies," she said, smiling like a rich donor who has just fed the children of the tenements, "I'm sure we are all very glad that these delightful people have come here today to interest themselves in the Lord's work and help so very practically toward the uplifting of the world. Now, wouldn't it be well to get right down to action? Mrs. Kingdon, will you repeat your motion which you made a little while ago before we were interrupted, so that everyone will understand?"

But before Mrs. Kingdon could get to her feet, Persis Dewy sprang up, her face white with anguish.

"Madam President," she said, her voice sharp in its intensity, "before such a motion is put to the meeting may I remind you all that we have a commission? And under our commission it would not be possible to even consider sending out a missionary who is not unquestionably a Christian with but one object, and that to preach Christ and him crucified as the only Savior from sin."

Persis Dewy paused for lack of breath, and Mrs. Searle, whose stare had been growing more and more coldly presidential, lifted her eyebrows inquiringly and said as sternly as her coral lips could frame the syllables, *"Commission?* I was not aware that we had a commission! Nobody informed me of any commission."

"It is printed right in our constitution." Miss Dewy's lips were trembling now. She had much ado to keep the tears from her eyes.

"Oh, *really?* But I don't happen to have a copy of the constitution. Won't you just read it to us, please, Miss Dewy?"

"Change the commission! Rewrite it!" called out Mrs. Kingdon in her hoarse voice. "That can easily be done afterward if we find it necessary. Madam President, I really think we ought to get this finished up. It is getting late and many of us have to leave in a few minutes."

"Just a minute, Mrs. Kingdon," said the president, trying to be diplomatic. "I really think we should get this matter clear and settled. Won't you read that commission, Miss Dewy?"

Miss Dewy had been fluttering through the pages of her secretary's book and now brought out a printed folder, and triumphantly stood up to read. Her voice rang out a challenge to the astonished little assembly: " 'Go ye into all the world and preach the gospel to every creature.'

" 'Thus it is written, and thus it behooved Christ to suffer and to rise from the dead the third day; and that repentance and remission of sins should be preached in his name among all nations, beginning at Jerusalem. And ye are witnesses of these things. . . .' "

Miss Dewy read the words impressively, and then, lifting earnest eyes, she broke into speech.

"Madam President, with a commission like that,

how could we send one out who could not witness that Christ had saved her soul? Christ did not say that we were to go into all the world and teach all nations to plant potatoes or corn. Those things of course would often be done by any Christian mission-ary, and have been done always, but they would be incidentals, not the object of going. Christ did not even say, 'Go ye into all the world and give medicine and heal the sick.' He said 'preach the gospel.'

"And how would one dare do what Mrs. Kingdon suggests—rewrite that commission? There is a curse pronounced upon anyone who dares to do that. It says:

" 'If any man shall add unto these things, God shall add unto him the plagues that are written in this book. And if any man shall take away from the words of the book of this prophecy, God shall take away his part out of the book of life, and out of the holy city, and from the things which are written in this book!' "

There was a frozen silence as Miss Dewy finished breathlessly. Suddenly Mrs. Kingdon arose.

"Madam President, I think the time has come to cut short such foolishness. Everybody knows that those are only verses from the Bible and quite anti-quated. If Jesus were on the earth today it is sure he would never have spoken such narrow-minded words. The ideal Christ would be broader, more up-to-date. I have heard that there is a movement on foot to rewrite the Bible, and it does seem as if such a thing is needed, although of course I understand it is in traditionally lovely language and a few copies must be preserved as heirlooms. But if the Bible could be written today it would be quite a different matter. And we should never allow progress in great movements to be stopped by some little antiquated saying that was written in the days when wisdom and knowledge were in their very babyhood. I move, Madam President, that we return to the motion. Have I a second for it?"

"My dear," said the president, turning to Miss Dewy with a sweetly official smile, "those are only Bible verses, you know, and quite antiquated, not a commission that is binding upon us."

"But you don't understand," said Miss Dewy eagerly. "They are the words of Jesus Christ and were included in the constitution—we all signed our names to it. It reads, 'We, the undersigned, recognizing the above commission from our Lord and Master do solemnly pledge and band together—' That is the original page on which the charter members signed their names, Madam President, and we have at least twenty of those members present here this afternoon."

Mrs. Searle gave her an annoyed stare and then laughed outright.

"Well, dear me!" she said amusedly. "It seems there are other antiquated documents besides the Bible that we shall have to do away with before we can get on with really important matters. But, ladies, I certainly think that we need not hesitate to proceed with our business, in spite of this matter of the past that seems to be in the way. If we find afterward that it is necessary to reaffirm what we have done today with a second vote it will do no harm, and in the meantime we shall know just where we stand and can go forward with the work in hand without delay. I have no doubt that this document can easily be set aside. I will consult the session of the church. In the meantime, Mrs. Kingdon, will you kindly make that motion again? It is only a matter of raising the money quickly, you know, and of course we cannot afford to delay."

But before the lady in question could possibly get to her feet, the timid little Mrs. Ryder arose and spoke eagerly: "Madam President," she said, with an insistence in her voice that arrested the attention of everybody in the room. "I *must* say something! I had a little boy once. He was run over by an automobile. He knew he was going to die. He heard the doctor telling us, and he was afraid. Very much afraid! Then someone brought Miss Mary Lee to see him, and she told him about his Savior and the promise that he that believeth hath everlasting life. She talked gently and made him understand about it, and prayed with him, until he was happy and not afraid to die anymore because he was going to be with his Savior. And he told us he would be waiting for us in heaven, and he died happy. Mary Lee did that for my Johnny! That's why I want her to go as our missionary, and I promise to pray for her every day and give everything I can afford. But I could not vote for anyone to go out there to bring just education or agriculture, or even health to those people when they do not know the way of salvation." She fixed her earnest eyes on the annoyed president's face. "*You* might have to die, too, someday, Mrs. President! Would you want somebody to come and teach you how to make a better garden, or even how to keep your health when you weren't going to need it anymore? Wouldn't you want to know the way to heaven? No, I can't vote for any new kind of missionary society. I want the gospel of salvation sent to the uttermost parts of the earth, for other Johnnies, like my Johnny, who have to die. No, I couldn't vote for that other lady! I'd *have* to vote for *Mary Lee!*"

A gray look swept over Mrs. Searle's face as the woman spoke of dying, but she tried to laugh it off.

She lifted her hands with a helpless little gesture.

"Well, ladies," she said apologetically, "we seem to be up against prejudice. Perhaps it would be as well to let it all rest right here for today. After all, it's quite a matter of raising money. And if these good friends think they can get along without us, and raise the money it will take to send even a Mary Lee to India, let them try! We will give them one week! If they can by that time produce the needed amount for the whole year, why, let them do it, and we can go on and work somewhere where we are really needed. I think, however, a little judicious wire-pulling will bring this out all right. And I see no reason whatever why we should not go right on making our plans and securing our assistants, for undoubtedly when the elders of the church hear of this they will know how to explain it to our troubled friends, and make them understand what true progress is. It is always a little hard for *elderly* people to understand, but that is the way the world grows. Shall we just be dismissed now without ceremony? I

promised that this meeting should close exactly at
four o'clock, and it is now two minutes of four. Suppose we meet at this same time next week, when we
shall hope for a better united understanding of the
whole matter. Good afternoon!"

The new contingent drifted out on a breath of
laughter, stirring up perfume of costly kind, dropping a light word here and there. Then the older
members slid out quietly like frightened wraiths,
hardly daring to look at one another, troubled in
their minds, some of them still uncertain what it
was all about, fearful that they might have sat too
long on the fence.

The Old Guard came last, sadly, silently, walking
together up the street far behind the rest, not noticed by the crowd that had dispersed in limousines,
avoided even by the other old members who were
troubled that they had not taken a more decided
stand.

The Old Guard reached the Dunlap home, three
rooms in a plain house, two bedrooms and a sitting-
room-kitchen-and-dining-room in one. Chester, the
crippled son, sat in the window watching them curi-
ously as they entered. What had happened to bring
sadness to his mother who had gone out so joyously
a little while before?

Mrs. Dunlap led them into her own bedroom and
without a word they knelt around her plain little bed
and began to pray. Chester in the other room could
hear them, and he brushed the mist from his eyes as
the prayers went on.

They prayed, each of them, with a faith that

reached out and laid hold of the throne of God, and the two who did not live there went forth pledged to pray all night.

The next morning Miss Dewy went out early before her duties in the Public Library demanded her presence, and called upon various old members of the missionary society. And at noon instead of going to her lunch she called up more on the telephone. Late that afternoon they gathered by twos and threes at the home of one of the old members and had a prayer meeting. And the next day they met at another home and had another prayer meeting. Every day all that week they met to pray somewhere! And the last day every member who was alive and able to be out of bed was present!

And when the week was over they all hastened early to the church again, a half hour before the time set for the meeting.

But just as they were entering the door, Mrs. Ryder, the mother of Johnny who had died, came hurrying to join them, a light in her face.

"I have something to tell you," she said eagerly. "I have been baking gingerbread every day and selling it to get a little money together for today, and yesterday my husband came in while I was taking the last batch from the oven and wanted to know what I was doing. So I just told him all about it. He got interested, and asked a lot of questions about it. And by and by when we went up to bed he said, 'Lyddy, I'd like to send that Mary Lee out to India. How much does it cost?' 'Oh,' I said, 'John, it costs a great deal! It costs even a little more than the big stone you were going to put in the cemetery lot for our Johnny,' and I told him what we had to raise. He was still a long time and then he said: 'Lyddy, what say we just put plants on Johnny's grave another year or two and take the money we'd saved for that stone to send Mary Lee to India? Wouldn't our Johnny like it better to have Mary Lee in India teaching people how to die, than to have a big fine stone over him?' and I cried and said, 'Yes, John!' So we talked it over and I've brought the money! It won't be quite as much as we need, but I thought perhaps God would send the rest somehow."

And then each one opened her purse and took out her savings, and when they counted it there were *fifty dollars more* than they needed to send Mary Lee to India!

Down on their knees went the Old Guard, and all the faithful old members with them, and praised the Lord.

They were praising the Lord when the president and her satellites walked in, praising him in such clear ringing tones that the social interlopers paused in dismay, not knowing just how to break up a prayer and praise meeting like that! Not until Mrs. Kingdon walked in, and said in her hoarse voice: "For sweet pity's sake! Don't let's put up with any more sob-stuff. Let's get down to work!" And the president at her instigation announced a hymn. She hadn't remembered to look one up beforehand. She announced the first one the book opened to and sang away without having any idea how appropriate the words were.

*God moves in a mysterious way, his wonders to
    perform.*
*He plants his footsteps in the sea, and rides upon
    the storm.*

But the Old Guard sang fervently from the heart.

The routine business went through without a
ripple, save for Persis Dewy's honest minutes which
her righteous soul could not help couching in caustic
language, especially the part about the great commission and the suggestion that it be rewritten.
Then the meeting came to attention and the president turned a honey-sweet look toward the Old
Guard.

"Now, ladies," she said, especially addressing the
former members who were grouped close together
today, "I believe the first thing on the docket is to
inquire whether there is any report from our objec-
tors of last week. Mrs. Dunlap, you were the first
one to object to our new plans. Can you tell us
whether anything has been done about raising the
money to send out a missionary from the church?"

Mrs. Dunlap arose with almost regal bearing and
answered quietly, "It *has*, Madam President."

"It *has!*" stared the president. "What has been
done, Mrs. Dunlap?"

"The money has been *raised*, Madam President!"

"It—*has* been raised?" asked the president in
astonishment. "How much, Mrs. Dunlap?" There
was a note of doubt in the president's voice.

"The entire amount, Madam President, *and fifty
dollars over*," said Mrs. Dunlap, trying to keep the

note of triumph out of her voice and sensing the tense stillness that hovered over the room.

"You mean, I suppose, you have secured *pledges* to that amount?"

"No, Madam President! We have *the cash*."

The air was fairly electric.

"May I ask," said the president after a second's hesitation, her voice taking on an accusatory tone, "just what *influence* you used to secure this sum in such a short time in these days of depression?"

"Yes, Madam President. We went to our heavenly Father, knowing that the silver and the gold are all his, and the cattle upon a thousand hills. We asked him and he sent it to us. The main part of it he sent to us through the father of the little child whom our Mary Lee taught how to die, but each of our members has had a part. And we have not asked a soul for a cent, not anyone but our heavenly Father."

The president gripped the desk and seemed to be bewildered at first, but rallied as she saw Mrs. Kingdon rise to the situation.

"Madam President," said Mrs. Kingdon grimly, "I think these good women should be commended for getting together so much money, *no matter how* they did it! And now I think we should try to get together with them and combine our forces. You see I have been inquiring and I find that it will take quite a little more to send Miss Melville to India than it would some less prepared young woman, and this sum that these good women have got together will nicely fill out our budget so that we can go before the board and not be ashamed. And now I feel that we should make it quite plain to these good friends who did not seem to understand last time, just what a wonderful young woman we are sending, and how well she will fit into a reconstructed program of missions."

Suddenly Mrs. Dunlap arose.

"I just want to make the ladies understand very plainly about this," she said in a kind but firm tone. "This money was raised to send *Miss Mary Lee* to India, and will not be available to send any other person. Neither will it be diverted to any other cause than the one originally planned by our society and Mrs. Bonner."

Then arose quite a babel, beginning with gentle persuasion, running the gamut of laughter, sarcasm, sneers, and scorn as the time sped away, and the new president was not getting anywhere with her argument.

At last Mrs. Searle drew herself to her full dainty height and said that unless this thing could be arranged amicably she would be obliged to resign. But lo and behold, when the matter came to a vote the Old Guard and their followers outnumbered the new contingent by enough to make a quorum, and the new president found herself confounded.

She made as graceful a retirement speech as she could frame on the spur of the moment, and lightly, with a haughty little smile, came down from the platform and went out of the room, followed by her satellites, Mrs. Kingdon bringing up the rear.

As she reached the hall door Mrs. Kingdon turned and looked back and spoke in a harsh voice.

"Ladies, you will find that you have made a very grave mistake, but I just want to say in leaving that you have convinced me more firmly than ever that the most dangerous thing we can do for the poor heathen lands is to introduce any more such narrow, bigoted views as we have seen exhibited here today! Good-bye, and I hope you find out before it is too late how foolish you have been, for this society will surely be on the rocks before the year is out!"

"Yes, on the rock Christ Jesus!" answered Mrs. Dunlap joyously.

"Praise the Lord!" said the little woman whose Johnny was in heaven by the grace of the Lord Jesus and the witness of one Mary Lee.

There was an automobile accident that night, and Mrs. Lansing Searle was thrown over an embankment and terribly injured. She lay a broken thing among silken coverings, and stared death in the face. She had made them tell her that she was going to die, that she had but a few hours to live. No one will ever know all that passed through her anguished mind in those hours. But at last there came the vision of the plain little timid woman in the missionary meeting and her story of the little boy who had been afraid to die. And then that startling sentence, "*You* might have to die someday, too, Mrs. President!" And Mrs. Lansing Searle remembered Mary Lee and her sweet, sure faith.

It was long past midnight when they sent for Mary Lee, sent a great limousine to bring her, and begged that she would hasten, for the time was short.

Mary Lee entered the great mansion where the Lansing Searles lived, and trod the velvet stairs, her heart crying out for the right word to give this passing soul. Her face was filled with the look she would wear someday when she pointed other sinners in India to the cross of Christ, her eyes seeing not the luxury about her, but only looking to Christ for help.

She knelt by the dying woman and took her soft white hand that already had the chill of death creeping over it.

"I've got to die and I don't know God!" wailed the woman who had been so self-sufficient.

"But God knows you," said Mary Lee gently. "He's always known you and loved you. He sent his Son to bear the penalty of your sins so that you might go home to him without a spot or blemish or any such thing."

"Oh, I've got to meet God, any minute!" moaned the weak, shrill voice. "And he knows what my heart has been toward him! I'm afraid!" She wailed agonizingly.

Gently the sweet tones answered: "It's not that we loved him, dear friend, for we didn't, but that he loved us! While we were yet sinners Christ died for us!"

Tortured eyes looked out between bandages, wonderingly.

"Oh, I'm a sinner, a great sinner. I know it now." Her voice grew stronger with earnestness. "It's not murder and stealing and lying that make one a sinner. It's just not wanting God in your heart. It's wanting your own way—*that* is unforgivable!" Again her voice broke in a sob.

"No, that is already forgiven, too. Listen! 'All we like sheep have gone astray, we have turned every one to his own way, and the Lord hath laid on him'—on his Son Jesus Christ—'the iniquity of us all.' Dear Mrs. Searle, if you put your trust in that fact, that God has done that for you, you need have no fear, for he says, 'Your sins will I remember *no more.*' You are accepted by God in his Son. You are just as dear as his own Son to him. How he will welcome you to his arms!"

"But won't I have to be judged for my sins?"

"No, listen! These are Jesus' own words: 'Verily, verily, I say unto you, he that heareth my word, and believeth on him that sent me, hath everlasting life, and shall not come into condemnation; but is passed from death unto life.' If you have heard the word of Christ and believed what he says, you are saved. Do you believe?"

"Oh, I have to believe. I didn't think it was so but now I see it. It is different when you come to die."

"Well then, dear, don't you see the question of a believer's sins was settled once for all on the cross when our Lord Jesus Christ received in his own breast the judgment that was our due? The believer cannot come into judgment for the reason that Christ was judged in our stead."

"But don't I have to do anything?"

"Just believe. Look! If I said I wanted to give you this little Testament, what would you have to do to get it? See, I am holding it out to you."

"Why, take it."

"Then will you take his salvation?"

"Oh, I will. *I must.* There is nothing else!"

"Well, then, let us tell him so," said Mary Lee.

So she led the dying woman straight into the presence of her Savior on the words of prayer, introduced her and handed her over into his loving care like a lost, frightened guest who had wandered away from the mansion to which she had been invited, like an alienated child from the Father's home. Pleading the claim of God's great promises, pleading the death of Christ upon the cross, pleading his shed blood, she brought her beyond the shadow of a doubt into safety and security.

Mary Lee's voice broke in a joyous sob, and as she opened her eyes she saw slow tears steal from the closed eyes of the sufferer and a light of peace spread over her face.

"Oh, it's true!" cried the dying woman. "Why didn't I see it before? But I was too full of myself to listen. Jesus! *My* Savior! He *is* my *Savior!*"

"Isn't it blessed," thought Mary Lee, as she watched the look of peace growing deeper, "that it doesn't take time to know God!"

Then she bent lower to hear the faint whisper that came from the dying lips. Those lips that but a few short days before had called the Bible an antiquated book were now asking: "What was that you said, Mary Lee—at the meeting? 'None other name'?"

Mary Lee quoted solemnly: "There is none other name under heaven given among men whereby we must be saved."

"Yes—that's it! Mary Lee, you tell those women —tell them I was *mistaken!* Tell them—there is no *other name!*"

Her voice trailed off into silence and Mary Lee thought she was gone, but suddenly she roused again and started up from her pillow, groping out as if she could no longer see: "Mary Lee! Mary Lee!" she cried. "Where are you? Mary Lee, you go to India and—*preach the gospel!*"

THE HOUSE
ACROSS THE HEDGE

IRIAM, humming a happy little tune, hurried about her morning tasks, washing the dishes, shaking out the cloth and folding it carefully, sweeping the hearth and the front door stone.

Occasionally, with glad anticipation in her eyes, she glanced out of the lattice to the house across the hedge; the hedge which separated her father's yard from the handsome grounds of the rich, influential Egyptian whose daughter Zelda was Miriam's dearest friend.

That hedge was also the dividing line between Goshen, where Miriam lived, and great, alluring, glittering Egypt where Zelda lived; but a hard-beaten path ran from door to door, and a distinct space in the hedge showed where the children of both houses had been wont to go back and forth from babyhood.

Miriam turned from gazing out the lattice as her

mother came in from the garden with a basket of herbs.

"Mother," she said eagerly, "I've finished everything now and I'd like to go over to Zelda's right away. She's giving a party tonight, Mother. A wonderful party. And she's invited Joseph and me. She wanted us to come over this morning and help her prepare."

Miriam's eyes shone like two dark stars. Her mother watched her with growing dismay as she put down her basket. "Oh, I'm sorry, dear," she said gently, "but you two mustn't be away from the house today!"

A stormy look came into Miriam's eyes. "Oh, but Mother, you don't understand! I must go. This isn't just an ordinary party. It's a dance, and there is to be an orchestra from the city, and caterers. A great many people are invited, the sons and daughters of officers high in authority. It is a great honor that we are invited. And you needn't worry about having to get me a new dress to wear. Zelda is going to lend me a lovely new one of her own, green and gold with crimson threads in the border. It just fits me and I look wonderful in it. There is a gold chain, and armlets and anklets of gold to wear with it, and Balthazar is getting me flowers from a real florist's to wear in my hair. He said, 'You will be the prettiest girl at my sister's party.' He has asked me to dance with him. Really, Mother, don't you see I must go? And Zelda's father has been so kind to my father, putting him into a better position. It wouldn't do to offend them."

"Miriam, I'm so sorry, dear child!" said her mother steadily. "But we are having a solemn feast tonight. God has commanded it. And you will have to be here!"

"Oh, Mother!" cried Miriam in desperation. "Why do we have such a tiresome, solemn old religion? I wish we had a religion like Zelda's. I went with her to the temple once. There was music and laughter, and dancing and flowers. Mother, why would I have to be here at the feast? Nobody would miss me if I stayed away."

"God would miss you!" said her mother seriously. "Listen, Miriam, we are going on a journey tonight! There is much to be done. It will take every minute to get ready."

"Oh, Mother! You've been talking about that journey a long time but we haven't gone yet. Why do you think we are going tonight? Zelda's father says that Pharaoh never intends to let us go, and he is close to the throne and ought to know. But anyway, even if we were allowed, Mother—why do *we* have to go with Israel? What do we want with a promised land? Why can't we stay right here? We have a nice home, and Zelda's father would always see that Father had a good place. He might even get something to do in the palace. Why can't we stay and be Egyptians, and take the Egyptian gods for ours? I'd like that so much better, Mother!"

"Stop, Miriam!" said her mother sharply. "You are speaking blasphemies. Don't you know that our God is greater than all gods, that he is the *only true* God? Oh, my child! I have sinned! We were told to keep our children separate from all other peoples lest they forget their God who has covenanted with them. We are a chosen generation, a royal people! We should not mingle with the world. And I have let you grow up in close companionship with these Egyptian children! That of which we were warned has come to pass! My child is wanting to leave her God to serve those who are not gods at all! Oh, I have sinned!" she sobbed. "I thought there was no harm while you were little children, and you begged so hard to play with them! You were so little! I thought when you grew up you would learn to understand!" She lifted her tear-wet eyes and spoke earnestly. "Miriam, you must never speak this way again. It is sin!"

Miriam stood sullenly with downcast countenance, still looking out the window toward Egypt.

"Well, anyhow, Joseph is going!" she pouted. "I heard him tell Zelda he would be over early to help Balthazar. They are going to the woods to get flowers to deck the house. And if Joseph goes I don't see why I can't go. He is only a year older than I am!"

The mother gave her a frightened look.

"He must not!" she said. "You don't understand. He must help your father all day. And he must not be away from the house tonight! There is danger outside of our door."

Miriam gave her mother a quick, startled look. "What do you mean—danger?"

Her mother faced her earnestly, sadly. "My dear, I haven't told you yet. I dreaded to bring you sorrow. Moses was here last night after you were asleep. He told your father that God is sending another plague—the last one. It is coming tonight. And then we are to go."

Miriam turned away impatiently. "Oh, those horrid plagues!" she said angrily. "Zelda's father doesn't believe that Moses has anything to do with them, nor our God either. He says they just happen! But anyhow, Mother, those plagues don't come to Goshen. Our cattle didn't die, and our men were not sick. When the dreadful hailstorm came that spoiled all the gardens of Egypt it didn't touch us. Zelda's father says we just happened to be out of its path. And don't you remember when that awful darkness came, it was all light in Goshen?"

"But you, my child, are wanting to go out of Goshen tonight of all nights! Listen, my child, though it breaks your heart, I must tell you. This plague is different from all others. Our God is passing through Egypt tonight to take the eldest son in every house. Only where he sees the sign of blood on the door will he pass over."

Miriam stood with suddenly blanched face, her hands clasped at her throat, a great fear growing in her eyes. "Oh, Mother! Not *every* house. He wouldn't take Balthazar, would he?"

"He said every house," answered the mother sadly. "From the house of Pharaoh upon the throne, to the house of the maid behind the mill. Those were his very words."

"Oh, Mother, not Balthazar! Don't say he will take Balthazar! Why I was to dance with him tonight! And he is sending me flowers!"

Suddenly down the path came flying footsteps. A

tap sounded upon the door, and Zelda, bright-faced and eager, burst into the room.

"Why don't you come, Miriam? You promised to be over long before this, and where is Joseph? Balthazar says the sun is high and the flowers will droop if they are not picked right away. Won't you call Joseph, and you both come at once?"

"I—can't come, Zelda," murmured Miriam, white-lipped, lifting eyes brimming with tears.

"You can't come? Why? What is the matter? You promised! I am depending on you."

"Zelda—something has happened! We have—a feast—tonight. I did not know about it before. And —we are going on a journey. But—oh—Zelda! It is something more than that! *Another plague is coming tonight.*"

"Another plague! How silly. I thought I had you all over that nonsense. How could you know a plague was coming, and why should that make any difference anyway? Are you a coward? We can take care of you if anything happens, though I don't believe it will."

"You don't understand, Zelda. This plague is different. Our God will pass through Egypt, and take the oldest son from every house unless the sign is over the door."

"How ridiculous!" laughed Zelda, with a sneer upon her lovely face. "My brother is well and strong. What do you think could happen to him between now and tomorrow morning? I told you all your family were superstitious, and now I know it. There! There is Joseph now in the yard with your father! I'm going out to make him come home with me. He has common sense. He won't be afraid to come."

She turned toward the door, her gaze still out the window, but suddenly stopped and drew back, her hands pressing at her throat.

"Oh," she cried out in fright, "what are they doing to that darling little white lamb? Isn't that the lamb your father had penned up, the one without a single spot? They're not going to *kill* it, are they? Oh, why does your mother let them do that? That poor little lamb! I think they are cruel! Oh, see! There is blood!" She pressed her fingers against her closed eyes. "I cannot bear the sight of blood! It makes me feel faint!"

Then, opening her eyes almost against her will, she looked again. "Why are they dipping that bunch of hyssop in the lamb's blood? Why are they doing that? Miriam, do you see? They are smearing it all over the doorposts and over the lintel. Why doesn't your mother go out and stop them? What an awful thing to do! *Blood!*"

"It is our God's command," said Miriam solemnly. " 'When I see the blood, I will pass over you,' he said. It is to save my brother's life, Zelda."

Zelda looked at her scornfully. "How could blood on a doorpost possibly save anybody?" she asked.

"You tell her, Mother," said Miriam, suddenly dropping into a chair, her head buried in her arms on the window sill, her shoulders shaking with sobs.

"Zelda, dear, it isn't that blood out there that saves Joseph's life. That blood is only a sign of our faith in a promise made long ago. Our God promised

that some day he would send One who would be a
lamb slain for the sins of the world, and that through
his death all who believed would be saved. And so,
when we put this blood on the door at his command
tonight it is a sign that we trust in the blood of the
Lamb that is to come. We are putting ourselves
under the blood covenant, where we know we are
safe. Do you understand?"

Then Miriam rose earnestly, with clasped hands
and pleading eyes looking into the angry, startled
face of her friend. "Oh, Zelda, won't you go home
right away and ask your father to kill a lamb and put
the blood on your door? For perhaps God will see it
and will pass over your house too, and your brother
will be saved! Oh, won't you, Zelda?"

But Zelda met her with hard indignant eyes a-
blaze. "What! Put blood on our doorposts when I am
going to have a dance? Why the guests would soil
their beautiful garments! Now I know that you are
not only superstitious but crazy! I hate you! I never
want to see you anymore," and she dashed out of the
door and down the path toward her home.

All day long as Miriam went about her work with
tears raining down her white cheeks, her heart was
aching with sorrow. As she prepared the bitter
herbs for the feast, and made the unleavened bread,
her eyes kept turning toward the lattice that looked
over to Egypt hoping against hope that perhaps,
after all, Zelda had told her father. Perhaps before
it was too late he might bring a lamb and put the
needed sign upon his door also.

But the day went steadily on and she did not see

him. The afternoon was on the wane. The house was
full of the smell of roasting lamb. The clothing was
stacked in convenient bundles for sudden going. Father and brother brought the sheep and cattle from
the fields, and neighbors hurried by doing the same,
their faces filled with grave apprehension.

Miriam, as she laid the table for the passover
feast, kept looking out the window toward the house
across the way. She saw the caterers arrive, and a
little later the orchestra carrying their instruments.
She choked back her tears and wished that she dared
pray to the God whom she had neglected.

Lights were springing up in the big house. Guests
in bright garments were arriving. Once she was sure
she saw Balthazar standing in the open door, silhou-
etted against a blaze of light, directing the servant
of a guest about his camel. Her heart leaped up with
great longing to go and beg Balthazar to do something before it was too late! But it was too late now,
with guests arriving over there for the dance, and
the feast about to be served in her own home. Too
late!

The passover feast was ready. The roasted lamb,
with the bitter herbs and unleavened bread, was set
upon the table. The relatives had arrived who were
to eat the lamb with them. They were all gathered
about the solemn meal, and Miriam's father lifted his
hands to ask a blessing on the feast. Into the hush of
that moment broke the music of the orchestra in the
Egyptian house, and when Miriam lifted her eyes
she could see the bright lights and the moving figures as the dancing began.

The night went on. The solemn feast came to a close. The midnight hour drew near and Israel waited with a hush of awe upon her homes.

Miriam, suddenly glancing up at her brother Joseph, saw a look of wonder and exaltation upon his face such as she had never seen before. He was like one who has been set apart from others by some great act. There was a solemn beauty in his face that filled her with amazement.

Then her heart suddenly stood still. For the orchestra across the way crashed into utter silence, and into the foreboding hush caused by its ceasing there came frightened voices, frantic calls, and she could see hurrying forms running hither and thither. A light sprang up on the housetop where she knew Balthazar had his room.

Then, into the listening night, there rose a cry of anguish such as never had been heard before, reaching from the house across the hedge to the next house, and the next house, and the next, all across the borders of Goshen. Egypt weeping for her sons whom the death angel had taken.

As they listened, with white faces lifted in awe and fear, there came a sound of footsteps flying down the path. The door burst open without ceremony, and Zelda burst in, her arms laden with bright silken garments, and her hands filled with chains and bracelets and jewels.

She rushed up to Miriam. "Here! Take these, Miriam," she cried with anguish in her eyes. "Take them quick, and ask your father to get the people to go quickly! Oh, Miriam! My brother—is—*dead!*"

Then she turned and fled back to her desolated home.

Solemnly the procession moved along. Out into the night went Miriam. Out under the far cold stars. Out toward the Red Sea and the wilderness, and a grave in the wilderness. Out following that pillar of fire!

Miriam in her place in the march was glad of the darkness to hide her tears. For every step of the way this one wish beat itself into her soul: "Oh, if I had only told them about our God before it was too late! If only I had *lived* the faith which my fathers believed! Ah, if I had *had* a faith of my own to live; I might have led them to believe also! But how could I teach them when instead I was walking in their ways?"

And then, suddenly, Miriam understood why God had commanded his people to be a separated people, his peculiar people, a royal generation, not expected to find their joy in the things of the world about them. It was because they had been called to higher, better things, promised by him whose word could not be broken—and the promise was sealed with blood!

THE WEDDING GARMENT

ARTHA WORTH came out of her house one afternoon in early spring, hesitated a moment on the doorstep, looking up and down the street for a taxi, and then decided to walk. At the last minute her car had developed engine trouble. If she waited for repairs she would be late to her various appointments. She hated to be late. She prided herself that she had so systematized everything about her that her life moved as on oiled wheels.

She was meticulously dressed. Every item of her costume was carefully considered and in perfect harmony with every other detail. Martha was always ready with her garments for each changing season as it came.

Her dress was just the right shade of brown cloth trimmed with flat cream-colored fur, altogether the most correct thing for that season. The chic little hat of imported brown straw with its two creamy gardenias under the tilted lacy brim was most becoming, and exactly matched the smart little brown shoes, as the soft doeskin gloves exactly matched the fur jabot about her neck.

If she had any makeup on her face it was so skillfully applied that even a connoisseur was left in doubt as to whether it was not just natural perfection.

Martha stepped gracefully down the street, fully conscious of her own charming appearance, and more than one woman from car or bus or sidewalk, or even hidden behind a sheltering window drapery along the way, watched her with envious eyes, and longed to be like her.

Inside her dainty purse was a gold mounted tablet on which were written her engagements for the afternoon. She was to read a paper at a missionary meeting at half past two. It contained a careful study of the topography of Mohammedan lands, intricate and accurate statistics of the cost of maintaining missions, and the comparative number of natives Christianized. She had figured to a fraction just how much it cost to Christianize each one. The paper would take twenty minutes to read and she had carefully arranged to have it placed first on the program after the opening exercises so that she might slip out and meet her other engagements. She was due at a committee meeting of a charitable organization at three-thirty, and she hoped to be through with that by four. With good management she ought to be able to stop at the orphanage and perhaps drop in to Judge Warren's office to see that poor widow who ought to have a pension, before appearing at the

Verlenden-Braithwaite tea for a few minutes. All these engagements fitted well together and her costume was quite right for all. A trifle more than was necessary for the missionary meeting, perhaps—there would be only a few quiet, plain old ladies there, who would scarcely appreciate the cut of her imported ensemble, the real distinction of her whole outfit. Still, that was the beauty of costly simplicity. It did not look out of place anywhere.

As she walked down the pleasant street she was thinking of her plans for the coming week. How well she had arranged them. The dressmakers were coming just before the Barnwell wedding in plenty of time to finish her new lace dress. It was a little awkward having had to ask that Mrs. White on Sylvan Avenue to change time with her. But of course Mrs. White wouldn't be going to that wedding.

She turned into the main avenue now where there were plenty of taxis. But it was only five blocks farther, and she had plenty of time, so it was hardly worthwhile taking a taxi.

But even as she glanced at her wristwatch to make sure, a prankish breeze took liberties with her delicate hat, pulling her hair out from its precise arrangement about her lovely forehead, and tossing her jabot full in her face.

Martha looked up annoyed and discovered the sky suddenly overcast, and a drop of rain fell into her eye. April, of course. But how unexpected!

Another and another great drop splashed down. Her new ensemble! Would the cloth spot? She started to run, but the wind caught her on one side and the rain on the other and ran with her. All the taxis seemed suddenly to have fled from the avenue. She cast about for a quick shelter and backed into a convenient doorway.

There were others scurrying for this shelter also, many of them, and they crowded her inside the doors. She found herself in a church entrance with the big audience room just behind her, its doors standing wide and people crowding into the seats. There was a meeting going on, but it was not her church.

People were crowding her more and more. A man closed a dripping umbrella directly over her Paris hat and someone stepped harshly on the toe of her lovely new shoe.

"If you will step inside and take a seat you will not be in danger of getting so wet, Madam," said another man in a damp overcoat. Martha retreated into the far corner of a back seat.

Suddenly the audience burst forth into music, and the gladness of it was almost annoying.

Jesus may come today,
  Glad day! Glad day! —

She shuddered involuntarily as she drew back into her corner under the gallery. What a startling, unpleasant thought to be flung into the orderliness of her spring day! It was unseemly, singing of the Lord in this familiar way. What a cataclysmic thing it would be to have Christ return to earth in the midst of the everyday work and program. How upsetting! She put the idea away with distaste.

The man who prayed seemed almost too intimate with God. Who were these people? Some peculiar cult that had hired the church for a conference, perhaps?

They burst into song again, every word distinct and clear:

He is coming again! He is coming again!
This very same Jesus, rejected of men—

There it was again, another hymn on that same theme! Could it be just a happening? But no, they were reading the Scripture: "In a moment, in the twinkling of an eye, at the last trump—"

Was it possible that anybody really took those words literally? *Now? Today?* How incongruous!

What was this meeting into which she had stumbled? A fanatical convention? She looked about the audience room, crowded now to overflowing. There were many people whom she knew, people of wealth and culture, some from her own church. Why, there was Judge Warren up toward the front of the church! And there was Mary, her dear friend! Mary was a saint. Mary was not a fanatic. Could it be that Mary believed such queer things, or had she, too, come in just for shelter from the rain?

Her meditations were arrested by a strong, tender voice from the platform:

"We know that our Lord Jesus is coming back to earth in visible form, first because he said he would: 'Let not your heart be troubled. . . . If I go and prepare a place for you I will come again, and receive you unto myself.' "

Martha sat up startled and began to listen, an anxious little frown between her eyes. She had earned a New Testament at the age of five for learning this fourteenth chapter of John, but never had she dreamed it had any reference to a literal return of the Lord. Outside the rain was pouring down, but she did not hear it. She was listening to this strange new doctrine. In all the years of her placid churchgoing twice a Sunday, she had never heard this doctrine preached before! Was it something new? Did people generally believe it? Passages of Scripture, words and phrases that suggested a possible coming of some One in the dim and misty future ages—she had always looked upon them as figures of speech, a fantastic picture language.

"The angels testified that Jesus would come again," said the speaker. " 'This same Jesus which is taken from you, up into heaven, shall so come in like manner as ye have seen him go into heaven.'

"And Paul gave his testimony later: 'In a moment, in the twinkling of an eye, at the last trump: for the trumpet shall sound, and the dead shall be raised incorruptible, and we shall be changed.' "

Martha shuddered, but the clear voice went steadily on repeating strangely familiar words that had never meant a thing to her before.

" 'For the Lord himself shall descend from heaven with a shout, with the voice of the archangel, and with the trump of God: and the dead in Christ shall rise first: then we which are alive and remain shall be caught up together with them in the clouds, to meet the Lord in the air; and so shall we ever be with the Lord. Wherefore comfort one another with these words.' "

Martha caught nothing of the comfort that these words were meant to be. She heard only the announcement of what to her seemed a catastrophe for which she was unprepared. She sat up sharply and listened with a startled pink spot glowing on each cheek as the verses multiplied. The man was actually stating that one out of every twenty-five verses in the New Testament referred to the return of the Lord. Surely that could not be so or she would have heard other ministers preaching about it. Could this one be right and all the others wrong?

The speaker went on to unfold prophecy. Martha had never heard before that the fig tree in the Bible always typified the Jewish people as a nation. She listened in amazement as the speaker reminded his audience that Jesus, when questioned of the times and seasons, had told his disciples that when they should see the fig tree putting forth leaves they were to know that his coming was close at hand. Surely this was farfetched, she thought, to take this symbolic language literally and think that it had any reference to the present-day effort of the Jews to establish a national home in Palestine. The speaker even dared to state that one of the main reasons for the world war was that Palestine might be once more in hands friendly to the Jews. He reminded his hearers that as soon as this was accomplished the war stopped.

Martha cast a hasty indignant glance about to see how the rest of the audience received this startling statement about the great world war in which men died to make the world safe for democracy. Think of all those bronze tablets everywhere, and the marble triumphal arches bearing the names of heroes, all the knitting, and the Red Cross bandages, and going without sugar in coffee, just to give Palestine back to the Jews! Ridiculous! An impertinence! Surely someone would get up and protest at this. But everyone was listening in eager absorption. Even her friend Mary wore a look of rapt exaltation.

And now Martha's attention was caught again. In quick succession, like spirits out of the past, came other proofs of the near approach of the great event, history written hundreds of years in advance, that was being fulfilled to the very letter. The records of fulfillment, many of them, were gathered out of the daily papers, events of which she herself had read. She had already recognized the worldwide tendency toward confederation under one head, found among nations, corporations, and organizations of every kind. She had, in fact, written a paper recently on that very subject and read it before the current events section of the women's club, for Martha Worth was a well-read, thinking woman, known to be up to date on politics and international affairs. But this astounding speaker dared to affirm that this tendency must surely lead in time to the coming of a great superman, a world ruler, who should be none other than the Antichrist of the Bible.

Martha had to admit, as she listened to verses of Scripture, that the League of Nations had certainly been prophesied. She heard with increasing horror the words concerning the "Prince of Rosh," the ruling spirit of Russia, who would spread terror from the north. She suddenly realized the tremendous significance of the revived importance of Rome. She heard for the first time about the two seasons of rainfall in Palestine, the "former" or early rain, and the "latter" rain late in the year which had ceased long ago "according to the word of the Lord," causing desolation in the land. She heard the prophecy read that it would surely not return until the Lord's approach was near; heard how it had most amazingly returned within recent years, only a few drops the first year, a little more the second, until now it had attained its normal fall, making a great change in the fertility of the land, "according to the word of the Lord."

With bated breath, sitting far forward in her seat, utterly unmindful of the rain outside, or of her unfulfilled engagements, she listened to those astonishing words of Paul to Timothy:

"This know also, that in the last days perilous times shall come. For men shall be lovers of their own selves, covetous, boasters, proud, blasphemers, disobedient to parents, unthankful, unholy, without natural affection, trucebreakers, false accusers, incontinent, fierce, despisers of those that are good, traitors, heady, high-minded, lovers of pleasures more than lovers of God; having a form of godliness, but denying the power thereof."

Instance after instance of the fulfillment of these things occurred to Martha as she listened with troubled, unbelieving eyes fixed upon the speaker, while he made clear how these words fit the present time.

And then, education! Increase of knowledge! Mechanical inventions! Airplanes, automobiles! Why, it was extraordinary that the Bible prophecies had held promise of all this throughout the ages and nobody had ever noticed it before!

And lastly she heard about the apostasy of the church. That phrase never had meant a thing to her before. Indeed she doubted if she had ever heard it. Now it seemed blasphemy! She could not believe that the Bible had really said that about the church, the holy church, that it should become apostate! Why, if the church was all wrong, what was left? Surely the church was doing more than ever today! She had heard many preachers tell how it was making the world better and better.

But this speaker struck at many of the activities and organizations of the day that she considered as sacred as the Bible and the church itself. She grew indignant. There were the activities that made up her whole life! They were the things upon which she relied to make sure her heavenly calling!

Rapidly the thrilling address drew to a close with wonderful, frightening words of how Christ was coming first to the air to take away the true church, the church that was not apostate. That implied that not all church members, not even all active church members, would belong to the church invisible, the body of Christ, which eventually would be caught up to meet the Lord in the air.

Indignation and fear struggled in her heart as she listened to the description of what would follow the sound of that silver trumpet. The dead arising! Her eyes filled with sudden tears. A kind of horror seized her at the thought of being caught up that way with the dead! But they would be *alive*—and of course she would not want to be left out if such a thing were really going to be, if it really had the sanction of well thinking, right living people of God! Of course she would be one of those who belonged to the Lord. She had always been an active Christian worker. Why, she had always been present to teach her Sunday school class, even when she had been out at a party till two or three o'clock Sunday morning. Even when she had no time to study her lesson she had always asked the questions in the lesson leaf faithfully and told her girls to look them up for next Sunday when they couldn't answer them. Of course, she didn't always remember to ask if they had, but—well she had always been faithful to her Sunday school class.

With the last word of warning, "Watch!" ringing in her ears, she rose with the rest for the closing hymn:

It may be at morn, when the day is awaking,
When sunlight through darkness and shadow is
*   breaking,*
That Jesus will come in the fullness of glory,
To receive from the world "His own."
*   O Lord Jesus, how long, how long, ere we shout*
*   the glad song,*
*   Christ returneth! Hallelujah! hallelujah! Amen.*

Then, with a frightened hunger in her soul, she turned reluctantly to go back to her world.

She was halfway home before she remembered her appointments for the afternoon. The missionary meeting! It would have been over long ago! She looked at her watch, *half past four!* She could scarcely believe her eyes. She held the watch to her ear to make sure it was still going. Half past four! She had been in that odd meeting over two hours. The charitable association would have adjourned at four, and the orphanage visitors' hours would be over too before she could get there. Judge Warren had been in the meeting, so he would not be in his office and she could not go there. There was nothing of her afternoon's program left but the tea, and somehow she felt strangely out of harmony with the atmosphere of a tea. She had a longing to rush home to her Bible and try to look up some of those references the speaker had quoted, just to prove they were not there.

Of course it was all a hoax. Some kind of new doctrine that would soon be shown up as dangerous and disturbing. She wished she had written down the references, but they would surely be easy to find; they were so odd they would shout at one from the pages. She had a vague notion that one of them was in Job and another in Revelation, and weren't some of them in those little books at the end of the Old Testament that one could never find? But she had a concordance somewhere in her library. She would find them.

When she reached home she went to work at once,

not even waiting to take off her new hat and coat. She turned the leaves of her Bible rapidly. Revelation caught her eye, and suddenly she halted at a verse. Ah! Here was one they had missed at the meeting, but somehow it had a sinister tone. How had they missed this? "Behold I come as a thief. Blessed is he that watcheth, and keepeth his garments, lest he walk naked, and they see his shame."

A chill went through her. Garments! Would one have to prepare garments for such a time?

Martha had no knowledge of dispensational truth. She was not aware that Christ does not come to his own as a thief, but as a heavenly Bridegroom. She saw only that awful word, "I come," reiterated, and a foreboding filled her.

Turning the leaves rapidly again to the end of the book, she came on another verse: "He which testifieth these things saith: Surely, I come quickly! Amen." And then that lilt of an answer—so strange that anyone could feel that way! "Even so, come, Lord Jesus." But of course, that was for those who were watching, probably, and had their garments all ready. But she shuddered. That picture of walking naked before the assembled world at such a time was terrible! She must get rid of all these notions immediately. She would go and find Mary and talk it over with her. Mary was sane, and Mary was a saint. Mary would dispel this gloom. She must get into a better frame of mind before Tom came home.

So she put away her Bible and went to Mary's house.

Mary had just come home from the meeting and

was sitting with her Bible and notebook going over the references.

Mary greeted her joyously.

"Oh, you were out this afternoon, weren't you? Wasn't it wonderful! I tried to reach you after it was over, but somebody held me up, and when I reached the door you were gone."

"Wonderful?" echoed Martha in amazement. "Who is he? What is he? Mary, do you believe all that? Do really nice people believe it?"

"Believe it? You mean believe that Christ is coming soon? Why, of course. It is the blessed hope of Christians, dear. Don't you believe it? It is one of the articles of the faith of our church, you know. Most Christians throughout the ages have believed it, haven't they?"

"I'm sure I don't know," said Martha crossly. "I never heard of it before. That is, I never supposed for an instant that anyone took those verses seriously. I never heard a minister preach on it, and I've been going to church regularly since I was a child."

"I know," said Mary sadly. "It does seem as if many ministers are afraid of it. I wonder why? But lately, dear, I've been hearing it a lot. There have been several other speakers on the subject in the city the last month or two. One from Australia, this one from London, and two men from our own land."

"But do you really mean that you believe all that man said? You think Christ is literally coming to earth—and *soon?*"

"I certainly do!" said Mary with a solemn gladness in her voice and a light in her eyes. "Isn't it glorious!"

Martha studied her friend's face with troubled eyes.

"Well, then," she asked at last with an anxious sigh, "if that is really so, how would one go about getting ready? What would one—*wear* on such an occasion?"

"Oh," laughed Mary happily. "We don't have to worry about that. That's all taken care of. If we are his own, and included in that wonderful meeting in the air, our garments are all provided for us."

Martha stiffened with dignity.

"What do you mean, provided for us? I couldn't think of accepting a costume for that or any other occasion. No self-respecting person would. It would be like renting a wedding suit. I always believe in preparing for all occasions. A well-ordered person will be prepared for every emergency. My mother always kept a shroud in the house in case of sudden death in the family. But can't you tell me what would be expected? Isn't there something said about it in the Bible? I thought it was very odd that he didn't tell us how to be prepared."

" 'That I may be found *in him*,' " quoted Mary softly.

"Oh, yes, of course," said Martha sharply, "but I mean, *really*. Don't you know what we are supposed to wear? What is the material?"

"Oh, yes," said Mary quietly, "white linen, of course."

"Linen!" Martha looked annoyed. "You don't really mean linen—*handkerchief* linen, perhaps? But wouldn't that wrinkle awfully?"

"It's *righteousness*, you know," explained Mary gravely.

Martha caught at the word.

"Oh, I see," said she with relief. "Well, that's not so hard. Thank you so much. But I must be getting home. If this thing is really coming off soon, I'll have to get to work."

"But, dear," said Mary anxiously, "you don't understand. You don't have to provide a garment. Christ has provided it himself. He says—"

"But I tell you I couldn't think of accepting that. It may be well enough for some poor, sick, ignorant, incapable souls, but I take it he expects more of those who have been better taught. Doesn't it say something about working out your own salvation? Good-bye, I must hurry. It is almost time for Tom to be home and I have to look over the dinner table to see if the spoons and forks are all on. We have a new maid and she is always making mistakes. Tom does get so upset when the table isn't set right."

Mary stood at the door and watched her friend go down the street, repeating thoughtfully, sorrowfully to herself the words:

"For I bear them record that they have a zeal of God, but not according to knowledge. For they, being ignorant of God's righteousness, and going about to establish their own righteousness, have not submitted themselves unto the righteousness of God. For Christ is the end of the law for righteousness unto every one that believeth."

Martha went home and sat down with her Bible

and concordance again, looking up righteousness. Ah, here was a verse:

"I put on righteousness and it clothed me. My judgment was as a robe and a diadem."

That was comforting. She had always been praised for her good judgment.

And here was another in Revelation:

"For the marriage of the Lamb is come, and his wife hath made herself ready, and to her was granted that she should be arrayed in fine linen, clean and white, for the fine linen is the righteousness of the saints."

So, Mary was right, linen was a symbol of righteousness. And she, Martha, was probably accounted a saint, in the heavenly accounting. Saint Martha! That sounded good.

Martha sat for some minutes looking off into space, thinking over her own virtues, and the many good deeds that were against her name, until her husband came and she arose with a sigh of satisfaction, her gloom all dispelled.

Tom had brought a man home to dinner with him and they had a fine evening together. Martha forgot all about the happenings of the afternoon and her disturbed thoughts. Not until they had retired for the night and the lights were out did she remember anything about it. Suddenly she spoke out in the darkness:

"Tom, did you know there were people who believe that Christ is coming back to earth again?"

"Poppycock!" said Thomas sleepily.

"No, but really, Tom. Our church believes it. It's a part of the faith."

"Well, they've kept mighty good and still about it if they do," laughed Thomas. "Where have you been this afternoon? We'll have you putting on a white nightgown and sitting on a fence rail to watch for an opening in the sky pretty soon if you get started on such notions. Don't you know there were a lot of nuts who had that in their heads several years ago and went to the dogs over it? Sold all they had and nearly starved to death! Went crazy when it didn't happen the way they had planned! For heaven's sake, cut it out! I want to get some sleep!"

Martha said no more, but she couldn't stop thinking, so she began to consider all that she had done to make the world better. Surely she would not lack for material for the right garments. At last she dropped into an uneasy sleep.

Sometime in the night she thought she heard a distant sound, clear, sweet, *peremptory* like a trumpet! She sat up instantly in bed with the thought, "Can that be the trump of God?" It came again, more clearly, and she thought, "He is come and I am not ready!" What could she do quickly in this emergency? It was the first time in her life that she had been caught unprepared for any great event.

Then she thought she remembered two chests in the attic, carefully put away from dust and moth. One was labeled VIRTUES and the other GOOD DEEDS. She must get to them quickly and somehow array herself before it was too late, so she should not walk naked and be ashamed.

She thought she took her bedroom candle and crept softly toward the stairs. She must not waken Tom yet, not till she was sure. She dreaded his sarcasm. If this should turn out not to be the trump of God she would never hear the last of it!

In the dim, dusty attic she set down her candle on an old trunk, and opened the chests. First the one labeled VIRTUES. Yes, right there on the very top lay the diadem of her judgment, catching rays from the candlelight and flinging them back into her sleep-filled eyes. That would be lovely for a coronet. And there was her sweet temper lying next, a placid necklace of pearls. And her perseverance! That had brought her much praise from the church officers, though her husband would insist on calling it persistence. But it would stand her in good stead now, a soft, firm garment. Ah, she had accomplished many things for good purposes through that virtue. Next was a bright little gold girdle of truth, and anklets of churchgoing on Sunday, bracelets of kindness, feathers of smiles and pleasant words—oh, there was plenty of material here for adornment.

She turned to the other chest and took out her good deeds. There was a shining piece of golden silk that stood for adherence to the commandments, laced with a ribbon of blue and with fringe on the border. Oh, she had kept the letter of the law most scrupulously. And there was a piece of white linen. She seized upon it eagerly. That must be for the outer robe. Its border was made of cunning needlework representing the many things that she had done for church and state. A little intricate design of flowers and faces, and scenes from her life. There, for instance, was her Sunday school class, bright, happy young girls, and the boys who belonged in their crowd. How often she had gathered them for good times, always insisting that it should be in the name of the church, with allegiance to its outward forms. They danced along the border of that linen fabric in bright silk colors, their very expressions portrayed in detail. And then the procession merged into a scene more grave. These were the men who had come to her for work when times were hard, the ones she had fed and helped, the wives and mothers for whom she had found shelter and food and labor, the orphanage for whom she had begged dolls and toys, the members of her charitable organization who had done her homage, the people she had called upon in the every-member canvass; and mingled with them all the flowers she had provided for the church, for the sick, and the sad—a garland for the border.

Hark! Was that a nearer trumpet sound? With trembling hands she slipped the garments over her head, threw them quickly about her shoulders, and draped around her waist and shoulders the lengths of embroidered white linen, donned necklaces, bracelets, the diadem upon her forehead, slipped her feet into a pair of golden shoes wrought delicately of the adulation of her own small world, and stood ready, listening.

Another peal of silver sound came trembling nearer, and she snatched up an armful of white linen from the chest. Tom would need something at the last minute, and of course would look to her to provide it—blame her, perhaps, if it were not close at hand.

She stooped to pick up her candle and hurry down the stairs, for the silver sound was coming close now and filled all the dusty attic shadows with a thrilling wonder.

But suddenly a blinding light shone round about her, a light so great that it fairly overwhelmed her. She closed her eyes and could not look at first, but gradually she grew accustomed to the brightness, and knew that it was glory, God's glory. What was it doing here in her attic? Ah, God had seen that she was ready, dressed in her own righteousness. Saint Martha! Her heart swelled with pride! She lifted her head with new courage and looked at the glory. Lo, it was a mirror and herself reflected in it!

With pride she looked with open face to see herself. But—what was this? A poor, frightened, ghastly face, a gaunt figure draped in tattered, soiled garments, dirty, besmirched, disgusting!

She put a trembling hand down and felt for her linen robe, ran a quivering finger over the embroidered border, watching herself in the glass to make sure it was herself she saw. Where were the golden threads that had been woven so cunningly among the flowers? Tarnished! Blackened! Spoiled! And the flowers were faded, their glorious colors sickly in the glory light! The linen itself was dirty and dropping in tatters! The brightness of his glory in the room showed all the destruction that she had not seen in the fond satisfaction of her own little candlelight.

She looked at her own image more closely now, with failing heart, and saw her very face and hands were thick with soil, the dust of the attic upon her brow, and in sudden humiliation and fear she dropped upon her knees.

Then a Voice spoke, out of the silence and glory: "All our righteousnesses are as filthy rags!"

The words went through her soul like a sword. She looked again toward the One who seemed to stand there before her, with his glory like a mirror, and saw the sin stains upon herself, saw that the filthy rags were unfit covering in which to appear before the Lord of Glory.

Then a strange thing happened. In the silence of that glory-filled attic, Martha knelt and began to understand that all things for which she had striven, all her former ideals, wishes, ambitions, pride, even her good works and virtues were worth nothing. There was only one thing worthwhile in the whole world, and that was to know Christ.

Suddenly, out of the memory of her childhood came words that spoke themselves to her very soul again with a new meaning that thrilled her as she had never been thrilled before:

"But what things were gain to me, those I counted loss for Christ. Yea, doubtless, and I count all things but loss . . . that I may win Christ, and be found *in* him, not having mine own righteousness, which is of the law, but that which is through the faith of Christ, the righteousness which is of God by faith."

Then all at once the room was filled once more

with the soft silver sound of trumpets, and golden angelic voices began to sing:

When He shall come with trumpet sound,
Oh, may I then in Him be found!
Dressed in His righteousness alone,
Faultless to stand before His throne.
  On Christ the solid rock I stand,
  All other ground is sinking sand.

THE DIVIDED
BATTLE

THE forces of darkness had been quietly working in Morningtown for months. At last they were drawn up in the open with shining armor, glancing sabers. Appalling hosts—file after file in battle array! Something had to be done about it, and done quickly, or Morningtown would disappear, its Christian citizens would fall before the onslaught of the enemy, and the witness which had been established in their score or more of evangelical churches would be wiped out.

On the ramparts of heaven, bright angels were watching, numbering the hosts of darkness, turning eager eyes toward the Christian people of Morningtown to see how their faith would stand in this great testing, waiting for orders from the Throne. Here and there an angel could be seen through the golden mist of the heights, winging his way downward on an errand of vital importance to Morningtown.

Overnight Morningtown had come to the knowledge of the invasion. Dark sleuths had been seen for sometime, it is true, skulking about the streets, talking with some of the weaker of the saints, winning one here and there; but the right-minded people of the town had not taken the danger seriously until the army was actually upon them.

The Reds, the peril from Russia? Oh, yes, the Bible mentioned that in a vague way, and overzealous Bible students had occasionally made a brief ripple in the monotony of placid Christian minds by suggesting that the prophecy concerning the Prince of Rosh who should come down from the north and spread peril might be actually upon them; but for the most part the Christians had smiled and gone their way. It might be that sometime something like peril could come from such things, but it wasn't in the least likely that disaster in such crude form could come today in a civilized world. The nations would of course rise and prevent it. Some even asserted that all this talk about Communism was bosh. What was the matter with Communism? There were good things about Communism, weren't there? Of course, new things were always denounced for a while till people got used to them. Even Russia wasn't so bad.

"They say the people of Russia are very happy, and have things so beautifully regulated for them," said one sweet Morningtown matron, whose life was one long idle hour in which she did exactly what she pleased.

The gangsters? Oh, yes, of course, but gangsters didn't show themselves much in Morningtown, at least not until last week when a Morningtown lawyer had been abducted on his way to his office and a hundred-thousand-dollar ransom demanded. But that would soon be cleared up.

"Kidnapping ought to be punishable with death!" asserted a dapper businessman who hadn't been able to believe at first that the man had really been kidnapped.

"Why, certainly!" answered his wife and two women who were calling upon her. "But to think those wicked men would *dare* do a thing like that in *Morningtown!*"

Politics were beginning to seethe, even in Morningtown. The wrong man had been elected in a recent campaign, and was driving wedges here and there in the security that had heretofore hedged Morningtown. Licenses granted for horrors unheard of before in the quiet town had suddenly awakened smug, satisfied citizens. People were beginning to say that *something* ought to be done about it.

New cults had stolen in unaware, so subtly that people thought they were merely bright new forms of trite old worship; yet now they began to make inroads into the ranks of the orthodox faith. And when the state of things began to affect the finances of the churches, *then* the churches sat up and took notice. *Then* the ministers of the churches met together to consider what to do to combat the forces of evil that had come in.

It was early fall and the ministers had just gotten home from their vacations. They were feeling rested —some of them—and fit and ready for work. Most of them considered that it would be an easy matter to rout the enemy. So, at the call of one or two who were not so complacent about it, they had come together to consider what was to be done for the common protection and good of the community.

The meeting was held in the largest and richest church of Morningtown. It was called early, at nine o'clock, with a practical program in the morning, consisting of reports from the different districts of the city as to the devastation wrought in each quarter during the summertime.

The women of the Old First Church were busy in the basement preparing a luxurious luncheon for the noon hour adjournment. The afternoon program in the early hours was to consist of suggestions from various representative groups. Later they would consider some set plan of action prepared by a committee who had called the meeting. The committee was chaired by one, Curtius Goodwin, a man beloved by many. The evening was to be devoted to a great mass meeting to arouse the community to the need for fighting, and to announce plans.

Meantime the enemy were encamped over against Morningtown ready for battle. An attack was imminent and the angels were assembled on heaven's ramparts to watch the struggle and join in the triumph song.

Down in the basement kitchen of the church, Mrs. Green, Mrs. Bartholomew, Mrs. Jansen, and Mrs. Ridgeway were cutting up chicken and peeling potatoes.

"It's good we didn't try to have chicken salad today," said Mrs. Ridgeway, plopping a couple of drumsticks into the big kettle that stood before her on the table. "Men do hate cold dishes on a cold day, and see how really chilly it has turned since the storm last night."

"But chicken salad is a lot easier to serve," said wiry little Mrs. Jansen. "You don't have to bother keeping gravy hot. Oh, you're making soda biscuits, aren't you, Mrs. Green! That's nice! I always say stewed chicken isn't worth eating without lots of soda biscuits and gravy."

"We're having a regular spread today, aren't we?" said Mrs. Bartholomew. "I wonder why? What is it all about, anyway? I just got home last night and found a note my daughter-in-law had left for me saying they wanted me down at the church early this morning. What kind of a meeting are they having upstairs, anyway?"

"Oh, I don't know, really. Something about an evangelistic campaign, isn't it?" said Mrs. Ridgeway. "I suppose that Mr. Tupper of the Fifth Church is putting it on, and trying to get the rest of the churches to finance it. He is so officious, isn't he? I suppose he is a good man, but he has such a long lugubrious nose, and he is always wanting special prayer services and things. They say he is very spiritual, but somehow I never liked him. When he prays he always gets to crying and the tears drip off his nose. He doesn't wear awfully clean collars either."

"Now, Mrs. Ridgeway, how do you know the tears

drip off his nose if you are praying as you ought to be?" laughed Mrs. Green, mixing her baking powder and flour carefully.

They all laughed playfully.

"Oh, well, I don't see any great virtue in just keeping your eyes shut if you don't feel prayerful," said Mrs. Ridgeway amusedly, "and I never do when that man is praying, he sounds so sanctimonious."

"They say he gets a terribly small salary," put in Mrs. Jansen thoughtfully. "I suppose maybe he can't afford to have a washerwoman very often. He has a sick wife."

"Well, poor ministers shouldn't marry sick wives!" said Mrs. Ridgeway firmly. "And anyway, a man like that has no business in the ministry! Of course *he* wouldn't get an adequate salary, a man like that, with tears dripping off a long nose! I wonder the other ministers let him dictate, calling meetings together for somebody else to finance! I wonder they put up with it."

"But I heard it was Curtius Goodwin who called this meeting, not Mr. Tupper at all," said Mrs. Green.

"Well, it's the same thing. He's an elder in Tupper's church," said Mrs. Ridgeway. "You'll find Tupper's at the bottom of it! He always is of anything queer!"

"But they do say that Mr. Tupper is very spiritual!" said quiet little Mrs. Bowen who had just come in and was tying on a large gingham apron over her neat house dress, preparatory to shelling peas. "They say he is deeply taught in the Scriptures, too, and the people in his church love him dearly!"

"Oh, good morning, Mrs. Bowen!" said Mrs. Ridgeway, looking up from her chicken. "Are you on this committee, too? I thought you had your turn last spring."

"I did, but Mrs. Clark is sick and she asked me to take her place."

"Well, that's good. You're one of the best workers we've got, if I don't agree with you in your choice of spirituality. I've no objection to Mr. Tupper's spirituality if he stays in his place, but when he attempts to tell ministers like our Dr. Patton when it's time to have special services, I draw the line! Imagine a man like Mr. Tupper trying to manage men of the intellectual development of Dr. Patton! It's ridiculous! They're not in the same class."

"Say," said Mrs. Green lowering her voice a little and looking toward Mrs. Bowen, who was hanging up her hat and coat on a hook at the far end of the dining room, "I heard that people think our Dr. Patton is getting awfully modern. Had you heard that?"

"Well, if he is, I'm modern too!" snapped Mrs. Ridgeway, adding a handful of chicken wings to the pot. "I certainly think he's a better guide than that Mr. Tupper. But he isn't a modernist. I heard him say he wasn't! Probably the people who said he was didn't know a modernist from a stick of wood. I wonder if they are going to have an evangelist or just have the preachers take turns? It seems to me in these times of depression that they ought to consider expense. If they have an evangelist there'll be that continual harping on money, money, money! I for one haven't any money to give to anything extra! And I can't see why they need an evangelist or special meetings either."

"They do say the town is getting awful!" said Mrs. Green. "I guess they need it, all right, especially since liquor has come back."

"Nonsense! Pessimism. The town isn't any worse than it ever was, and it's all a lot of propaganda, I say! People like Mr. Tupper want to get into prominence, so they get up an idea that the town needs saving just so they can be great heroes and save it! They want to get their names connected with some big evangelist or great public speaker and have people ask them to pray and things, and get their pictures in the paper as being foremost in running the campaign! I know *one* at least who is always prominent in these things who generally gets the job of handling all the *money* that comes in. I guess you all know who I mean. I'm not mentioning any names." Mrs. Ridgeway slid the final piece of chicken into the pot and set it on the stove, carefully adjusting the gas flame to suit her need, amid a significant silence in the room. There were quick, furtive glances and lifted brows. Then she came back to wipe off the table for the next act.

"I wonder," she went on, "who they'll get if they have an evangelist. I'm sure I hope they won't try having that old Mr. Banning they had last summer. Of all the sob stuff! It was just the limit!"

"I heard they were thinking of asking Dr. Garthwaite. Wouldn't that be simply great? They say he's the most cultured speaker, and has the reputation of being the best Bible teacher this side of the water," offered Mrs. Spicer, who had just come in and was taking off her hat.

"Well, I guess that'll run into money," said Mrs. Jansen. "They say he never goes anywhere under a hundred dollars a night!"

"*A* hundred!" said Mrs. Ridgeway. "Better say *three* hundred, or even five sometimes! The idea of any man thinking he can preach even *a* hundred dollars' worth in one evening! In my opinion, any man who makes merchandise of the gospel isn't fit to preach! For my part, I'd like to have that Mr. McClain they had over at Craigstown last winter. He was interesting and good looking, and real snappy, and what's more, he knew when to stop! I hate these long, drawn out *appeals*. For my part, I would only be turned against religion if I were an unconverted person."

"I heard that Mr. McClain didn't get on well with his mother-in-law," offered Mrs. Green as she rubbed the shortening into her flour. "*I* think a man who can't get on with his own relatives hasn't any right to be preaching the gospel."

"Well, there *are* mothers-in-law!" laughed Mrs. Bartholomew, looking significantly toward Mrs. Spicer who had the reputation of nagging her daughter-in-law, though there wasn't a better worker, nor a more ardent member of the missionary society in the whole church.

"Well, Mr. McClain has a fine mother-in-law," said Mrs. Green eagerly. "My mother's cousin knows her well. She lives next door to her and she says she's perfectly *lovely*. She's the most saintly Christian she knows!"

"Do you mean that sickly looking Mrs. Faber?" snapped Mrs. Ridgeway. "My word! If you call *her* a Christian I'll give up! She has a tongue like a pair of manicure scissors. I'll own she can run a meeting, but there's plenty that can do that and haven't any more Christianity than my foot! For sweet pity's sake, don't judge an evangelist by the way he treats his mother-in-law!"

"Well," said Mrs. Green with an offended air, "I'm sure I don't care to go to the services if they have that man. I should be thinking of the way he treats that sweet little woman all the time. You can say what you like about her, but *I* happen to *know* her!"

"Yes, and so do *I!*" snapped Mrs. Ridgeway, slamming off to the dish closet and beginning to hand down piles of plates.

"Well, I wish they'd get that Mr. Brown from London. They say he's coming over this year and if we tried we could get him first of anybody. They say he's just *won*derful!" said Mrs. Jansen. "I'd like to hear somebody for once that had a big reputation like that!"

"Oh, but I heard he wasn't sound," lisped Mrs. Trevor, a pretty, golden-haired, glib-tongued young woman. "I heard he didn't believe in future punishment—I *think* that was it—or perhaps it was safety and security—or else he *didn't*, I'm not sure which it was, but I know they thought he wasn't sound. People in Morningtown would never agree to have him if he wasn't considered sound."

"Oh, but he *is!*" said Mrs. Green. "I heard the elders talking about him the other night. They say that's just something some enemies of his have got up about him."

"If there's any question there's *no* question!" said Mrs. Ridgeway severely, arriving back in the kitchen with her hands full of teaspoons. "What do you think, ladies, these teaspoons are all sticky! Can you imagine it? Who was on the committee last time? Mrs. Randall? I *thought* so. For my part I'd rather have less prayers and more cleanliness. The next time I hear her leading in prayer with that smug little holy smile and her eyes shut so sweetly, I'll think of those sticky teaspoons!"

There was a general laugh at this, and then Mrs. Green held up a warning finger to her lips.

"Sh!" she said under her breath. "There comes Mrs. Holmes. She's always scolding people for gossiping."

"Hm!" said Mrs. Ridgeway under her breath also. "She's not so holy as she looks! I heard her talking to the milkman this morning out the back door—she lives in the other half of my house—and my word! If that's Christianity, lead me from it!"

Mrs. Holmes advanced into the room smiling.

"Oh, there are a lot of you here already, aren't there? Well, I'm glad. You won't need me for a little while, will you? I do want to run upstairs to the gallery and listen to the devotional meeting. That minister from the new nondenominational church is going to lead it and they say he's perfectly *wonderful!* Why can't you all come? There's plenty of time. I'll come right down as soon as it's over and work hard. I was to set tables and there's plenty of time for that!"

"Thanks awfully!" said Mrs. Ridgeway curtly. "I prefer to stay here and do my duty. Besides, I'm not crazy about any fledglings just out of seminary—or Bible school. I guess he didn't even go to seminary, did he? They say he can't speak correct English. I heard he says 'lay' instead of 'lie'!"

"Oh, the idea! *Really?* I believe I'll run upstairs just a minute. I'd like to see what he's like!" said Mrs. Trevor, untying her frivolous pink and blue beribboned apron.

"*I* heard," said Mrs. Bartholomew when the significant smile that followed Mrs. Trevor's hasty exit had begun to fade, "I heard that the minister they have over at Exeter First is *divorced.* I wouldn't like to have a minister who was divorced, would you? It seems somehow unministerial, don't you think?"

"It seems unchristian!" snapped Mrs. Ridgeway. "I shouldn't care to listen to a man who upheld such standards. What would our country be coming to if the Christian religion closed its eyes to divorce? I wouldn't think a man like that ought to be allowed to sit in and vote with a body like what's meeting upstairs. I wonder if the other ministers know it?"

"Depends what they were divorced for!" said Mrs. Spicer slicing tart apples into the pie she was building.

"You don't even know he *is* divorced!" suggested Mrs. Jansen. "It might not be true. Anyhow, I think you ought to wait till you find out for sure before you condemn him."

"Where there's doubt there's usually *no* doubt," said Mrs. Ridgeway, primly shutting her thin lips. "Juliana Green, did you scald those kettles before you set the potatoes to cook in them? You can't trust the way the last committee washed up, remember."

Upstairs the devotional meeting was over and there was a little stir as the surreptitious attendants in the gallery stole out one at a time, through a swing door that needed oiling, and the ministers came to order to consider the program of the morning.

The ladies burst into the basement again with renewed vigor in their manner.

"That perfectly stunning new minister over at Third is there," said young Mrs. Trevor, fluttering into a chair and beginning to shell peas daintily. The peas were almost shelled and there was a possibility of an end sometime in view, so she chose to shell peas.

"He has the handsomest eyes!" she babbled on, "and they say his wife is darling! She's very active among the young people and shows them all sorts of good times at the manse. He preached at the open air meetings in the Park all summer and I just adored hearing him. They say his wife is very liberal."

"Yes," said Mrs. Green, "I guess she is. Mrs. Brown told me that she had a bridge party at the manse the other night. Three tables! Imagine that for a minister's wife! I'm glad she's not our minister's wife!"

"That's not so!" said Mrs. Holmes majestically, turning on her victim sternly. "I happen to know it's not so!"

"*How* do you know?" asked Mrs. Ridgeway.

"Because I *asked her,* if you want to know!" Mrs. Holmes' voice was calm. There was deep condemnation in the look she turned on Mrs. Ridgeway. "Mrs. Blynn who lives across the way from her came and told me that same tale you're telling. She said, just as you did, that there were *three* tables. She said she *saw* them playing. Three tables! And I said I *knew* it wasn't so. I happened to know that minister's reputation. I happened to know he and his wife are both opposed to worldly amusements, so I just went in and *asked* her."

"You went and *asked* her?" echoed Mrs. Trevor delightedly. *"What* did she say?"

"You went to the manse and *asked* her?" echoed several other ladies.

"I went to the manse and asked her!" responded Mrs. Holmes impressively. "And she just laughed. She sat down in a chair and laughed and *laughed,* and then she explained that her sister and her two cousins and their husbands had driven over from Ulster County and brought them a big new picture puzzle, and they were putting it together. She said they had used the little center table and the cutting table and the small table from the hall so there would be room enough for everybody to work at it, and they had the picture divided into three sections. It was a very large picture. She said they had a good deal of fun over it and sat up till they finished it, and that it took a long time. But she said she guessed she'd have to pull the curtains the next time she played with a picture puzzle."

There was a dead silence in the room for a moment, and then Mrs. Ridgeway with pursed lips said, "Well, I don't know but a Christian can waste as much time fiddling with a picture puzzle as playing bridge. I for one haven't any time for *either*. It's frivolous, especially in a minister! I really don't care to hear men preach who do foolish things like that!"

Said Mrs. Holmes with dignity, "It's high time the tables were set! Where are the tablecloths? Are you sure we have enough? There are a lot of men upstairs. I could run home and get a couple more tablecloths if you think we need them."

"You'd better stay here and *work*, if you ask me," said Mrs. Ridgeway grimly. "If there are more people up there than were *invited*, the rest of them can sit at bare tables, provided there's anything left for them to eat. Personally I have no time for these Christian scavengers, running anywhere they can get a meal for nothing!"

Then those women went swiftly to work setting the tables, and the pleasant clatter of dishes and pans covered their further conversation.

Out in the basement hallway, a couple of dark shadowy spies from the ranks of the enemy encamped about the town, stole silently, unseen, up the stairs, well satisfied with what they had already heard, one to listen further upstairs in the church, the other to hasten to his military head and report progress.

This was his report:

"So far all going well. The company hastily assembled from the ranks of Morningtown Christians to prepare for battle are already turning their swords against each other. Christian casualty list quite satisfactory. Many noted ministers, Bible teachers, and women of saintly reputation among the slain. People still blindly fighting each other, under the impression they are attacking the enemy."

The ministers came down to lunch well pleased with their own activity. They had heard the reports about the enemy in their midst with gravity, but they had little doubt that they would be able to cope with the adversary as soon as they were thoroughly organized. They all told a good many jokes and funny stories, and laughed immoderately as they devoured the chicken and biscuits to a wing, and added mashed potatoes and pickles and peas and tomato salad, and apple pie a la mode, washed down with cups and cups of coffee. All, that is, but a few of them who sat together conversing gravely with serious brows and earnest talk. They seemed almost sorrowful, and some of them scarcely bothered to eat, they were so absorbed and troubled.

The scout who returned to the enemy's headquarters at the close of the luncheon carried back a concise report of progress.

"Slaughter becoming general during noon hour. Many noted evangelists slain and their bodies thrown to the beasts of prey!"

During the afternoon session there were occasional surreptitious withdrawals from the audience, a minister here, an elder there, into the shadowy corners of the Sunday school room for quiet consultation. A careful watcher might have noticed that they were of the wealthier churches, and that the expressions they wore were not such as betokened peace and love. They talked by twos and threes in unnoticeable corners, and shook their heads meaningfully with sneering smiles. And when the plan of action drawn up and presented by Curtius Goodwin was read for approval, and came to a vote, these men mustered their forces for a protest.

One brother arose to plead for more time. He said there were many who would not agree that the evangelist selected was the wisest choice that could be made.

An elder went on to speak of two others on the list of speakers and cast slight aspersions on their spirituality and fitness for the honored task of leading Morningtown Christians on to the fight. At last all but a very few of the noble list of picked warriors lay wounded before the august company of Christians.

Discussion grew hot. Some very sharp words were exchanged. Some plain truths were told, and denied point blank, and a decision seemed no nearer than when the question was first proposed.

In the shadowy dimness back under the gallery two demon-emissaries of the enemy stood taking notes. One of them, young in his office, looked puzzled.

"I don't see how you tell which are Christians and

which are fighting for us," he said at last, in an aside to his superior officer, who was watching the argument with great satisfaction.

"Don't you know the rule?" asked the other sharply. "This is their own Leader's word: 'By this shall all men know that ye are my disciples, *if ye have love one to another'!*"

A look of surprised comprehension began slowly to dawn upon the young demon's face.

"Why, then almost all of these are fighting for us!" he said with a glance that took in the whole congregation.

"Yes, practically all of them, except a few that I seem to have lost sight of during the afternoon. I wonder if they have gone home? Come this way and let us look through the other rooms of the church. Not much account perhaps, but still it is my duty to watch them all."

They stole through the shadows and drifted here and there.

"I wonder what this door's shut for," said the young officer, pausing beside a closed door that opened into a classroom.

He listened a moment.

"Ha!" he said, and stole around into the adjoining room to peer through a crack where the partition had not been tightly closed.

"Put your eye to that crack!" he whispered. "I thought I'd find them up to something!"

The younger demon peered into the dark classroom and saw five men upon their knees praying. They did not appear to be great men; two of them were quite shabby, but they were praying mightily.

"What does that mean?" said the younger spirit, stepping back.

"It means," said the older one, "that they have a secret wire hidden somewhere over which they are sending messages back and forth to heaven. Didn't you hear them crying for reinforcements? And they'll get them, too—just those few plain men—because they keep in constant touch with their Leader. You don't find any of *them* wounding any of their own men. They have private information, and their eyes are constantly to God, their ears continually open for his guidance. We knew there was a leak somewhere and information was getting through our lines, but we couldn't exactly locate it. Now there are two other places I've got to watch and report about. Come on!"

He led the way down to the basement.

The luncheon was all cleared away and a supper was in process of evolution. The long tables were freshly reset. Platters of pink ham with parsley borders were at intervals along the tables, dishes of olives and celery, great plates of rolls, glass dishes of quivering jelly, lettuce-lined dishes of cole slaw, small dishes of squarely cut cheese. It was going to be a good supper. At every place was a glass of well-blended fruit cup, and out in the kitchen were great cakes being cut into generous slices, chocolate cake, fruit cake, coconut cake, sponge cake, pound cake, cupcakes, maple cake, custard cake, angel cake, and devil's food. It was a luscious array, and there were big freezers of ice cream.

But the two spies did not stop in the kitchen. The young officer cast a quick look about for three women who had been there an hour before. Finding them not, he went softly around, peering into little rooms that were used for Beginners and Primary Sunday school classes. At last in the farthest little room he found the three women kneeling in a corner.

"I thought so!" he said frowning, and wrote something in his little book.

"Now, come!" he said hurriedly. "There's a group of young people. I have to check up on them. They are here to wait on tables tonight and do some singing between the courses. They've given us a great deal of trouble this last year. They are comparatively new recruits, and such happy faces and joyous lives I've never seen. They've triumphed everywhere they've testified. We had to do something, so we've sowed dissent among them, turned their thoughts inward, showed them where they were being slighted, got them to see the faults of their friends. There was just no breaking up their fighting spirit before that, the way they were going on. They were meeting constantly to sing and pray, wearing radiant faces till everybody was asking why they were so happy. But we've had some of them on the run this last week. We'll see how they are tonight."

He pushed open a door that led into the church gymnasium, where stood about twenty young people in small groups, a girl and two boys, a boy and three girls, four or five girls. They were all talking earnestly, some of them emphatically. The two spies stepped near and listened.

"Well, she scarcely speaks to me anymore," a pleasant blonde girl with lovely wavy hair was saying.

"Why, Jeanette! I thought you all were wonderful friends. Wasn't it Mary and Fred who brought you to the Bible school in the first place?"

"Yes, it was," said Jeanette, her lip quivering, her eyes filling with sudden tears, "and we've always come together till two weeks ago. One night they just didn't come as usual, and they didn't send me any word, and when I met them the next morning they just nodded and never explained a thing. They haven't come to get me since, either! I waited for the bus that first night when I found they weren't coming, but it was late so I didn't go to class at all, and I've had to stay away ever since because the folks at home don't like me going all that long way in the dark to the bus."

"Well, I think Mary's jealous," said one of the girls earnestly. "I do, I really do! Fred's always so nice to all the girls."

"Well, he hasn't been nice these last two weeks," said Jeanette, turning away to hide her feelings. "But Mary couldn't have been jealous! She always sits with Fred in the front seat, and he always treats her as if she were the only person in the world, no matter how nice he is to us other girls."

"Oh, forget it, Jeanette," said one of the boys. "I guess Mary and Fred are out of fellowship. I heard they went off on a ride the other night instead of going to the meeting."

"Yes, Fred's going with those fellows down at the

Club again," sneered another lad. "I thought his conversion wouldn't last long."

The elder of the two spies lifted a satisfied face with a little smile hovering over his lips.

"They're all right!" he said. "There'll be more carnage tonight, if I don't miss my guess. Here, listen to these."

They drew near to another group of young people.

"What's the matter, Isabel? You haven't been coming down to the Bible class lately."

"Oh, well," laughed a pretty girl with a trifling beribboned Swiss apron over a frivolous dress, "I can't be bothered! What's the use anyway? I can't be good. I'm having too much fun. And since I found out that Tom Riley and his sisters go to dances, I don't see why I shouldn't have fun too. They're called such good Christians, and yet they do that! And I decided that probably every Christian is that way if you just knew. Awfully good Christians when they're leading a meeting, and do as they please the rest of the week!"

She laughed a mean little laugh.

"But you oughtn't to judge all Christians by what some do," protested a sweet, shy-looking girl, "and you oughtn't to judge Christ by what his poor, weak followers do!"

"Why not?" said Isabel sharply. "If he isn't able to make them different from other people as they sometimes claim, what good is it to be a Christian at all? Why not have a good time? Besides, I don't find any of them that don't say rotten things about some of

the rest, and when I found that out I was done. I'll
live my life the way I want to and I guess I'll come
out as well as the rest." She laughed carelessly. "I
just heard of a minister's wife who talks a lot of
gossip about the different church members. I don't
see that that is any better than going to dances. As
far as I can see I'm as good as anybody."

"But, Isabel, you're missing a lot," pleaded the shy
girl, "and the Lord *is* able to make his own children
different. It's just that we don't let him have his way
with us."

"I'm not missing anything I care about," said Isabel with a shrug of her shoulders. "Look at those two
over there, Tom and Hullie. They went to meeting
strong at first. Maybe they go now too, I don't know,
but I just heard them telling Anna Sears the rotten-
est story ever about Greta Long, and she was one of
those girls they used to pray for and take to meeting
with them."

The senior spy smiled triumphantly toward the
other.

"You see!" he said. "We've got them going. But
what are those young people going into that little
cloak room over there for? We must look into that."

He peered into a place where the paint had been
scraped off the ground glass.

"Ah!" he said, drawing his breath sharply.
"Another stronghold! That's one thing we can't work
against!"

The apprentice, peering in after him, saw three
young men and two girls down upon their knees

praying earnestly that God would be in the midst of the meeting upstairs and overcome the evil one. "Have thy way with us all, Lord," they heard one say. "Take us and break us and make us over! Mold us, fill us all with thy Spirit *at any cost!*"

The older spy flashed an angry look.

"I must go at once and report this," he said. "Something strenuous will have to be done about it. Now there'll be reinforcements from angelic headquarters. It's those words 'at any cost' that destroy all our weapons. Come! This must be known at headquarters at once!" And the two slid silently out of the door and into the world of darkness.

Over the ramparts of heaven the angels leaned anxiously watching, while the professing church of God romped on "according to the course of this world, according to the prince of the power of the air, the spirit that now worketh in the children of disobedience." Having their conversation in the lusts of the flesh and not in the spirit, fulfilling the desires of the flesh and of the mind, just as though they were still by nature children of wrath and had not been quickened from their deadness in trespasses and sins.

The church was full that night, though many who belonged to the objecting contingent remained away. In fact almost every man who had held up the decisions in the afternoon by disagreement and opposition was conspicuously absent. Yet both galleries were packed. People even sat on the pulpit stairs and stood against the walls.

They didn't mind that the church organist was absent. A young man from a visiting church went to the piano and fairly made it speak the words as he played.

Mrs. Ridgeway sat in wonder until suddenly the young speaker caught her interest and her conscience with his first words:

"Therefore whatsoever ye have spoken in the darkness shall be heard in the light: and that which ye have spoken in the ear in closets shall be proclaimed upon the housetops."

Suddenly Mrs. Ridgeway remembered some of the things she had said about a lot of people that day, and she gave a tired shiver and decided it was time to go home. She was in no mood for heart-searching. She considered that she had done well that day and she didn't want to be made to suspect that perhaps she had not.

But a lot of people crowded into the seat just then, and she couldn't get out without making a disturbance, so she sat still and the speaker went on:

"For we are made a spectacle unto the world, and to angels, and to men."

In his opening sentences he spoke of the great world war and how the boys who went out to fight were under the eyes of the whole world. How each nation was watching them and weighing their value as soldiers.

"The Christian Church is in a warfare today!" he said. "Only our warfare is in the spirit realm, not in the natural, not against flesh and blood! The Christian has been delivered from the natural realm, delivered from self, good self, bad self, religious self, and all the other kinds of self; he has been brought into another sphere, and it is in that sphere he must live and wage his warfare.

"We have been hearing all day of the enemy, encamped upon the very outskirts of this lovely town. We have trembled to think what has been going on while we have been asleep to the danger. Now we are met together to combine our forces against the prince of the power of the air. One of the first things we need to realize is that we cannot make a single move without orders from on high, because we are not fighting just for Morningtown. We are fighting one of the battles in the great war against the enemy and we are a spectacle not only for the other towns about to see, the other states, the other nations, other men, but a spectacle for angels. They are watching us there on the ramparts of heaven. And Christian warfare in order to be effective must be fought from a heavenly standpoint, not from the earthly or carnal standpoint. And that being the case, we cannot use carnal weapons, that is, worldly weapons and devices such as human organization, and the businesslike schemes the world would use. If we do we are neglecting the spiritual and losing the power that is of God. There must be spiritual warfare on spiritual ground, with spiritual weapons, or else we are defeated at the start.

"We are here as a church to take the prey out of the hands of the evil one, that sinners may be saved, saints built up, and a people prepared for the coming of our Lord Jesus Christ in glory and power.

"The Holy Spirit begins instruction about this warfare by telling us what it is not, and one of the very first things he tells is that our warfare is not with one another! The very moment Christians get to warring with one another, the church is divided. We fall into criticism, sharpness, unforgiveness, and bitterness, and we are defeated. The very moment Christians get into a state of judging or criticizing, with bitterness and unforgiveness toward one another, they are not only defeated in their own lives, but other people are defeated by their influence. And by the things they do and say, the devil is well pleased. He knows very well that if he can get the church of God to warring with one another they will not war against him."

Mrs. Ridgeway's cheeks began to burn as she sat with bright eyes fixed upon the speaker, every word he spoke condemning her own actions.

For it was not only the things that Mrs. Ridgeway knew she had said that day about other Christians that were cutting like a knife into her conscience as she listened. Mrs. Ridgeway had a sister-in-law with whom she had been at war for years. A good Christian woman she was, too, and Mrs. Ridgeway knew it. Yet she had condemned almost everything she did, until she had worked her brother into a state of uneasiness that had almost broken up his household and his Christian testimony. And it had all started about some trifling differences of opinion until it had become a serious matter.

"I can tell you why your prayers are not answered!" said the speaker, "why you are not having the sweet experiences that God wants you to have. If as you analyze your life and experience you find any tendency to judge other people, to criticize, to speak evil of others, to have a bitter, unforgiving spirit, that is the cause. God will have to judge you if you criticize others.

"God wants you to go after sinners, to be loving and patient with saints, and if you are sharp and censorious with others you will only drive them away from God instead of winning them. God wants you to show forth by your life—even if you cannot say a word—that he has done something, that he has saved you and separated you unto himself, and given you his own life and his own patience and grace.

"There are many Christians who are worldly and who have no power in their lives. When you walk with God, and his Holy Spirit has his way with you, keeping you every step of the way, then he will give you power and answer your prayers. Put yourself into God's hands at any cost to yourself. Then he can make all this real to you. He has left you here on earth that his power might be manifested through you to others.

"When we are fighting among ourselves we cannot prove God's weapons mighty in pulling down the strongholds of the enemy. The enemy is watching. The angels are watching. The world is watching. 'By this shall all men know that ye are my disciples, if ye have love one toward another.' No, we've got to get a Calvary heart, the heart that made the Lord

Jesus willing to go to Calvary for men, before we can fight against the enemy's strongholds. You've got to love your fellow Christians even if they don't agree with you about a lot of things.

"Brethren of Morningtown, before you go out to battle, get down upon your knees and ask God to show you yourselves. Then examine your weapons. Be sure that they are not carnal weapons. Put on the whole armor of God, 'and above all, prayer.' Pray that there shall be no more divided battle. Then go forth and prove that God's spiritual weapons are mighty to the pulling down of strongholds. And remember that not only men and devils are watching you, but angels are watching also and rejoicing over your victories."

The noted speaker had to catch a train as soon as the service was over, but the audience was hard to disperse. People stood talking with one another and saying with tears in their eyes, "That was wonderful! That was what we needed. That hit home to me."

Everywhere, all over the church, people were confessing to one another, "That sermon was meant for me!" And here and there a couple who had not been speaking came together and shook hands. One or two asked forgiveness of one another.

Mrs. Ridgeway from her place high up in the gallery stood a moment or two and watched, and then hurried down and away into the night, going straight to her sister-in-law's house.

"I've come to tell you I've been wrong, Rebecca," she said, twisting wry lips and snapping the words out reluctantly. But there was a tear in her eye, and Rebecca saw something more like humility in her face than had ever been there before.

Back at church a group dropped down upon their knees up near the pulpit, and began to pray, and others who had been standing in the aisles or by the door tiptoed up and knelt beside them. Incense of prayer arose as a sweet-smelling savor to the Lord, prayer that could be answered. Humble, contrite prayer, prayer that was filled with confession of sin. The kind of prayer that took hold upon the promises of God.

Then in a panic the listeners in the shadows fled. These Christians had forgotten their differences and had begun to pray! The battle was on and the God of battles was in command! It mattered not that the three most influential churches in Morningtown were not represented in that group upon their knees. The angels were not counting riches nor influence nor education. They were looking upon those who were utterly yielded to their God and ready to go to the forefront of battle with him.

Reinforced from above, Curtius Goodwin and his helpers went forward to the battle, fortified by constant prayer.

They did not draw up any finely worded petitions against the evils in the town, nor get up crusades. They were not fighting with carnal weapons. They did not even canvass the town to get voters against the gangsters. They established a prayer room in the corner of the great old tabernacle they had repaired and refurnished, and prayer was sent up continually, day and night.

"But I don't understand," said Dr. Patton one day, meeting Mr. Tupper on the street. "You made such a stir about how you were going to fight the enemy, and you haven't closed up one notorious place yet."

"No," said Mr. Tupper radiantly. "No, brother, we haven't bothered about cleaning up the places. The places are only the result of sin and lost souls. We are trying to save the souls. Had you heard yet, Brother Patton, that Dirk Sullivan was saved last night? Dirk, you know, is the proprietor of the most notorious gambling den in Morningtown, and Dirk is *saved!* That means that one gambling den at least is finished!"

"Saved?" said the good doctor raising his eyebrows. "Now, just what do you mean by the expression, Brother Tupper? You mean he has got emotional and come forward in your meeting? But how long will it last?"

"As long as eternity lasts!" said Mr. Tupper joyously. "No, Dirk didn't come forward. We didn't even know he had been to the meetings. He came quietly one night at midnight to talk with the evangelist who had been preaching that evening—" Mr. Tupper did not remember that it was the noted evangelist to whom Dr. Patton personally had objected in that first meeting, but Dr. Patton did, and winced a little—"and he told him he felt that he was a great sinner and he needed a Savior, but he couldn't believe that Christ had died for such as he. Then after the way had been made plain to him, Dirk Sullivan got down on his knees and prayed, and he told the Lord that his gambling den would never be open again. I went down there with the evangelist this morning and found him as good as his word. The gambling equipment was being burned, and the place scrubbed clean. He wants some of the young people to come down there tonight and hold a prayer meeting. He's bought some chairs and hymn books himself, and he wants to bring Christ where he formerly served the devil, he says."

"You don't say!" said Dr. Patton, rubbing away the mist that had come to his eyes. "You *don't say!* Well, I hope he sticks!"

But the angels were gazing in wonder at the manifold wisdom and grace of God.

THE
STRANGE GOD

THE Brandons had always been active Christian workers even when they were very young. Frank Brandon had been made president of the Christian Endeavor in his church when he was a mere boy; and Emily Fuller of the Epworth League in her church when she was very young. Both of them had sung in the choir, both had been most zealous in county and district work of all sorts. They were always being put on committees either in church or community work, wherever any activity was started along religious lines. Just as soon as anything was decided upon, someone would always say, "We'll get Frank Brandon interested in that and it will be sure to go like wildfire," or, "Put Emily Fuller in charge of that and there won't be a hitch in your arrangements."

And so when these two joined forces in marriage, everyone was marveling over their future, and the respective Fuller and Brandon contingents each began planning to absorb them both.

This of course was most pleasant and flattering to

them, and the result was that finally each took over many of the activities of the other, and became busier than ever, abounding in good works, with scarcely time to call their souls their own. But they seemed to enjoy it. They continued to take on new activities until one wondered how they did it. But they never complained of being weary. They seemed to thrive on the adulation of their friends.

"Oh, you two! You're simply tireless, aren't you?" an elderly member would say, shaking an admiring finger at Emily playfully, and sighing lazily. "You'll certainly have a lot of stars in your crown! I wish I were as good a Christian as you are! You'll certainly have your reward in heaven! How *do* you *do* it?"

"Oh, that's nothing!" Emily would say lightly, "I just love this kind of work. But, dear Mrs. Brown, *are* you going to make us one of your marvelous angel cakes for the sale? And *would* it be too much to ask for two quarts of your celestial salad besides? You know, if your name is on anything we can charge half again as much and get away with it. We do want to make enough to get a new church carpet. The old one is simply unspeakable!"

Mrs. Brown would always end by promising both angel cake and salad, and patting Emily on her exquisitely rouged cheek, saying, "What a wonderful little Christian you always were, Emily; I quite envy you your crown!" And Emily would dimple and smile and flutter across the aisle to beg Mrs. Peters for four quarts of her "heavenly mayonnaise" to put in little amber jars with her name hand-painted on the label.

It was just the same with Frank. "Frank, old man, we're putting on a comedy to help out with the mortgage on the church this year, and we want you for end man. Now there's no use in making excuses, for there's nobody who can put over the jokes the way you can, and we mean to have you."

Or the Sunday school superintendent would accost him. "Brandon, how about your taking that class of boys? They've had five teachers and finished them all, and the one they have now isn't a teacher at all. He just sits and lets them walk all over him. You could manage them, I'm sure. Get them interested in some class activity; basketball, or tennis, or something athletic, and make them feel some church responsibility. They can join the church leagues and play with other churches, win cups and things, that'll give them a church spirit! Why, those fellows ought all to be church members at their age! How'd it be if you make a rule that only church members are eligible to play in the interchurch games? Something like that, see? I'm sure you'd be just the one to start it."

"Good idea!" said Frank pleasantly. "I'm not sure, but I'd enjoy that if I can make the time. I can see possibilities. We could have weekend conferences in the summer up at one of the camps and teach them the latest methods of church work; raising money, etc., and give them a dash of church history, or maybe a talk or two on personal responsibility; something really serious. Then when they get home let them put on a church social, using some of the methods they've learned. We could give two or three prizes; one for the most original program, one for the best suggestion of how to raise money for the church, and—well—one for the best menu for a church banquet. Yes, I can see great possibilities. I'll think it over and try to make time for it. It sounds great to me!"

Things had been going on like this for several years. Frank had a great Bible class of boys—very many boys and very little Bible; and Emily had a like class of girls, whose chief business it was to get up new and startling ways of entertainment to hold the boys in the church. Visiting strangers, introduced to the Brandons and informed how wonderful they were, would respond with a wistful wish that they had some such workers in their church.

The church the Brandons attended was the most thoroughly programmed of any church in the city. The minister was wont to boast that the young people of his church had no need to go anywhere else for their entertainment, they had enough at home.

"Sorry, brother," Frank Brandon said when Harry Sharpless, an earnest young man from another church who was formerly a member of Frank's Bible class, suggested their joining in a city-wide movement for weekly Bible study. "Sorry, but we wouldn't have time to spare. Monday and Thursday nights we have our regular league games; Wednesday night we have practice in our own church gym. Of course that doesn't come till after the prayer meeting, but it breaks into the evening and no one would like taking on another date, for we require them to be on time at practice. Of course, the young people don't go to prayer meeting. But to tell the truth, some of them get into the gym while prayer meeting is going on and have a little practice on the side, so that hour wouldn't be available. Then Tuesday night our church orchestra and choirs meet, and a lot of our young folks belong to those. Friday night we have either movies or some kind of church entertainment, and Saturday nights we have our church "Get Together Club." Ever hear about that? It's quite unique. We have the whole church divided into sections and they take turns being hosts and hostesses. We have a supper connected with it, of course. We've just put in a miniature golf course in the basement of the church. The young people did the work themselves, and it's great! The old people sit around the fire and sing popular songs and the young folks play games. We have a couple of ping pong tables too. It's really great. Ever been over to see it? You ought to come. Of course we have a modest charge for outsiders to come and play. But I'd be glad to have you come as my guest sometime. You'd enjoy it and maybe get an idea of how to work something like it in your church. No, I'm sorry, Harry. I'm afraid we wouldn't be able to join you in that Bible study idea. And, you see, we really don't need it. Our young people are all hard at work in the church, and of course most of them come from Christian homes and we get plenty of that sort of thing on Sunday anyway."

It was the winter that they were putting on the missionary play that Emily stopped Rose Altar, a newcomer to the church, and asked her to come to a committee meeting that was to be held in the church parlor an hour before the morning session of Sunday school next Sunday.

"I'm sorry," said Rose, "I'm afraid I couldn't come at that time. You see, we always have family worship at that hour. Sometimes during the week we have to be hurried, but Father likes to take more time for it on Sundays."

"Family worship! How quaint!" said Emily, staring a little. "Imagine it! I didn't know anybody did that anymore. But couldn't you stay away just once? You see, we're putting on a marvelous play next month and we're assigning the characters. We want to begin to rehearse this week because we want to take all the time possible for preparation, and we thought we could just read over some of the parts and let you get the idea, and see what you were expected to do. We'd do it in the afternoon, only the church orchestra is giving a sacred concert then and a good many of us are in that. But anyhow, can't you come just this once? Tell your father it's *quite* religious. It's a sort of a pageant of all missionary lands. The costumes are gorgeous! They are ordered from abroad. The Mission Board is getting them for us. There's a dear little Mohammedan one that I think would about fit you. I know you would be stunning in it. We are hoping to do a lot of good with this play. It's the beginning of the great World Drive for Foreign Missions, you know, and it's marvelous what a prospect we have. We've already had three invitations to put the play on at other churches. If all goes well we rather expect to give it a good many times, in the suburbs, and even over in the next state. I wanted to be sure and get you to come in with us right at the start, for I have an idea you'll be awfully good."

But Rose Altar shook her head.

"I'm sorry, Mrs. Brandon; you're very kind, but I just haven't time for things of that sort."

"Oh, I'm sorry," said Emily a bit shortly.

She was stung and astonished that the sweet young stranger had not immediately recognized and followed her lead. She was not used to having any-one refuse her requests and invitations.

"Poor child," she said to herself, looking after her with an almost contemptuous smile. "She must be under the domination of a fanatical father. Fancy family worship! How quaint! How Victorian! Well, she'll come around, of course, when she sees it's the thing to do; but she'll have to take what is left. I can't run any risks waiting. She can be a Zulu girl, of course, if nothing else is left, though she may object to the bead costumes. However—I've done my best for her."

So the play went on and enthusiasm spread like wild-fire.

The Bible study classes went on also, and many unexpected ones were added to them—of such as should be saved. But there was a large number of eager, earnest young church members who would have come into the Bible meetings and enjoyed them, but they felt their first duty was toward the mission play that their own church was getting up. It was going to do so much good for foreign missions!

Frank Brandon, coming home from his office an hour later than usual one day in late February, swung himself aboard the train just as it was starting, and walked through three crowded cars, finally dropping into the only vacant seat he could find, the little single one by the door. He opened the evening paper. He was extremely tired and didn't want to talk, for things had not gone well. The first thing that morning his valued secretary had sent word that her mother was very sick and she couldn't come to the office that day. He had been obliged to hire a public stenographer. Then about ten o'clock word had come that the bank where he kept his prosperous account had closed its doors, cutting him off indefinitely, not only from his bank account, but also from the safety deposit box, which contained valuable papers and bonds which might be used for collateral. Besides, he had a headache and a sore throat and ached all over. His throat had been sore when he left home that morning in the sleet and slush, having forgotten his rubbers in his haste. He shivered as the draught from the opening and closing car door slithered down his collar. He felt miserably sick and remembered he had a meeting of the federated committees in the church that evening. He unfurled a newspaper more as a protection than because he wanted to read it. He didn't want to talk to anyone. He was not noticing his fellow passengers. His eyes were on his paper, though he was not much

interested in its news. The usual number of acci-
dents, murder cases, and a new suicide—Mather,
director of the bank where his money had been.
Well, what good did that do, committing suicide?
Coward! Thinking to slip out of his obligations that
way and leave the mess to other people! Well, of
course the man wasn't even a church member. He
hadn't any respect for himself. You couldn't expect a
man like that—

Suddenly he forgot to finish his thought, for he
heard his own name spoken by one of the two men
sitting just in front of him. He hadn't noticed who
they were, but now he recognized their voices. One
was Mr. Harris, a successful lawyer, as noted for his
interest in church affairs, as he was in his profession.
The other was Harry Sharpless. It was Harris who
spoke first:

"Did that man Brandon from the Fifth Church go
into your Bible conference work?"

"No," said the other, "he said he hadn't time!"

"Why, I'm surprised," said Harris. "I supposed he
was a live wire, always interested in church affairs.
With such speakers and teachers as you have secured I would have expected him to *take* the time!"

"Haven't you ever noticed," said young Sharpless
with a bit of a twinkle, "that Frank Brandon never
goes in for anything that he himself isn't running? He
just has to be the head or he won't play. And from all
I've seen his wife must be a good deal the same way.
It's a case of:

I love me! I love me!
I'm wild about myself!

I love me! I love me!
My picture's on my shelf!"

"Well, I don't know about that," said the graver
voice sadly. "I hadn't thought about it before. Too
bad, isn't it? He could be such a power. Do you know,
Sharpless, there are a great many self-worshipers
today who are going about most actively carrying on
service in their own strength, and for their own
sakes. They worship self under the impression that
they are worshiping God. That is the blinding of the
enemy, a part of the great delusion. Power, success,
without God! When all the time the Lord is saying:
'Not by might, nor by power, but by my spirit, saith
the Lord of hosts!'

"What a pity Brandon couldn't be present at some
of those meetings. Even one would be an eye-opener
to him, for I believe that at heart he is a conscientious young man, if he could only be made to see the
truth."

Frank Brandon shrank further behind his paper.
Cold angry chills ran down his back, and a sick
feeling came into the pit of his stomach. His feet and
hands were like ice and his face burned hot with
fury. Was this what people thought of him? Was it
possible that they so misjudged him? Admired and
successful though he had been, generous and ready
to help everybody, yet there were those who
thought of him like that! Of course it was jealousy. A
man couldn't expect to be popular and not have some
people jealous of him. But these were Christian people, prominent in church circles! Who would ever

have suspected them of such petty jealousy? Well, he was thankful that he had none of that! A scrap from the solo he had sung in church last Sunday rang through his memory:

God, I thank thee that I am not as other men!
I fast twice in the week,
I give tithes of all that I possess!

And they thought he was an egotist! Both of them actually agreed that he was always thinking of himself. That obnoxious song that Sharpless had quoted! He knew it. He used to sing it in college. His lips shut sternly. It was outrageous!

Well, he would just forget it, of course; that was the Christian thing to do. But somehow he must show those two that what they said was untrue. He really couldn't stand having anybody going around talking about him like that! Perhaps it would be a good thing to just lean over and challenge what they had said now, settle the matter right then and there and dominate the situation before those two went out and spread such an idea! That was the only way to handle such a thing. Prove them in the wrong, embarrass them, just lean forward and smile and ask them pleasantly—well—just what could he ask them? He couldn't merely get up and declare himself innocent of their charge. If they really had such a thing in the back of their minds, his word that it wasn't so wouldn't mean a thing. What proof could he bring that it wasn't so?

Then like a tantalizing little imp, the couplet ran through his brain.

I love me! I love me!
I'm wild about myself.

And something moved within him. Could it be that there was any truth in the assertion that he wasn't interested in anything that he himself didn't run? Of course people were always asking him to take over the management of so many things. He couldn't help it, could he, that there were so many things he was responsible for that he hadn't time for the rest? There! That was something he could ask those two! He would do it right away and see what they said.

But having made this resolve he suddenly felt that he must have a little more to say.

While he paused to collect a list of his good works wherewith to confound them, suddenly the two rose as one man, with the exclamation: "Why, there is Dr. Leveridge up there at the other end of the car. Let's go and speak to him!" and they hurried eagerly forward to greet a gray-haired, kindly faced man. Frank recognized him as one who had been pointed out to him a few days ago as a conference speaker.

Frank lowered his paper an inch and watched the eager meeting between the three men. He saw how their faces lighted. He was wont to see faces lighted with greeting like that for himself. Yet two of these faces held behind them thoughts against his reputation as a Christian! Of course Sharpless had been just a kid in his Sunday school class not long ago.

But a sick wave of fury passed over him. Somehow he felt left out, and he was not used to being left out.

He couldn't just march down the aisle and tell them he had overheard them talking about him. They hadn't even known he was there! But he could easily get out into the other car now while they were up front and they would never know he had been there. That was of course the dignified thing to do, and he had known it all the time, only his fury had made him impatient. He would go at once while they had their backs turned. He arose swiftly and slipped out the door, crossing the platform to the next car.

There were no seats in the next car and Frank had to stand on the platform by the door, swaying with the train and hiding his face with his newspaper. But it was a salve to his hurt feelings to know that there were several younger men in that aisle ahead of him who would eagerly have urged him to take their seats while they stood in the aisle or sat on the arm, hanging on his words, if they had known he was there. But he was not ready to talk with anyone just now. He had just received the shock of his life. It had never before entered his head that any one *could* talk that way about him. He felt a righteous wrath, with a great pity for himself, and felt he must get himself adjusted and decide what to do before he talked with anyone, even Emily.

He decided not to tell Emily anything about it. No need of her having to bear this, too. Of course young Sharpless had been the only one of the two who had said anything really mean. That awful song—"I love me!" It disgusted him more and more as he thought of it. What Lawyer Harris had said wasn't so bad, only he had in a way accepted the slur. Christian people! Talking that way about one who was doing twice as much Christian work as they were!

Well, somehow he must prove to them that they were wrong. How would it do to go to one of their old meetings? Let himself be seen in a front seat! Make it known that he was in thorough sympathy, only he had not been able to go sooner! That was a good idea. If he could get rid of this rotten headache and the aches all over him, he would go tonight. Of course there was a meeting of the federated committees tonight, but it wasn't important, and he could telephone to Sommers to take his place as chairman for once. Well, he would do it no matter how bad he felt! It was important to reverse this feeling before everyone heard of it.

When the train stopped at his station he swung off into the darkness, hurrying down the street to his home. He didn't take a taxi lest someone else would be in it. He didn't want to talk with anyone. His throat was raw and his head throbbing. He drew his collar up about his neck and bent his head against the wind and sleet. He knew he was in no condition to go out again that night, but he meant to go. It rather gave him satisfaction that he was going in spite of being sick. It had come to seem quite the most important thing in the world that he be seen in the front seat of the conference *at once*.

At home Emily protested, "Why, you are *sick*, Frank, and it's beginning to sleet! You're not fit to go out. Besides, you have that committee meeting. I was going to suggest that you call them up and have them meet here. Then we could ask their wives and serve coffee and cake afterward. I think that would be much more interesting."

"No," said Frank, "I've got to go to that conference tonight! I promised I'd look in on them, and this is perhaps the last night! Anyhow, it's important. There are reasons why I feel that I should lend my influence to it. And I'd like you to go along with me if possible! I really feel we ought! I find it's quite expected of us, and I guess it must be a good thing. They need encouragement. Poor things. They've got that great hall on their hands and I don't suppose it'll be half filled. We really should have gone earlier, taken hold of the thing somehow. It seems people think *we* ought to do *everything!*"

So they went to the meeting. When they turned into the street where the hall was located they wondered if there was a funeral somewhere, there were so many cars parked on both sides of the street. They had to go a block and a half away from the hall and walk back, and Frank had forgotten his rubbers again.

When they reached the hall, they were surprised to find people pouring in by the hundreds. They thought at first they must have gotten into the wrong place.

And there was no front seat to be had! Indeed there was scarcely a seat left anywhere on the street floor, and the galleries were filling fast. Men were already standing leaning against the walls. So Frank found a place for Emily behind a post where practically no one could see her, while he stalked up the aisle and took up his stand on his angry aching limbs at one side of the pulpit steps. He leaned against the cold, cold wall, and presently discovered there was a cold air ventilator right over his head that blew down his neck. But anyone who could see the platform could not fail to see him standing there, one foot braced on the lower step of the pulpit. There he stood with a haughty heart but a smile of patronage locked upon his face for the evening.

It was hard work standing there with his whole body aching like a toothache. The room was hot, for the audience was vast, and he was constantly conscious of his hot, dry, prickly throat. But as he gazed into the faces of that audience he forgot his own discomforts. In amazement he noticed people present who seldom attended any church. He wondered how they got them there? There hadn't been any special advertising! And there were familes, *whole* families, from all the churches, eagerly uniting in singing with a zest that showed they counted it a special privilege to be there. This really was something that he ought to have recognized, it seemed. Yet failing to find a response from him, the Lord had done it without him! He felt somehow aggrieved at God.

The singing astonished him right at the start; it was so tremendous, and the congregation didn't need to be worked up to it, either. There was an earnest man up on the platform holding them all in perfect time with an unobstrusive hand. He had a cultured voice with heartthrobs in its very timbre, but he seemed to be merely directing the great volume of sound that was not perfunctory, but came from hearts alive and singing unto the Lord.

Frank Brandon had conducted choruses himself that had been considered great successes. He had always felt he could bring out of an audience the utmost sound it possessed. But he had never heard such singing as this in his life. As they started on the second hymn, which was eagerly requested from the audience, he found there were tears in his eyes. But the words were almost startling. They were:

Empty me of self, Lord Jesus—

He looked around furtively, half wondering if Sharpless or Harris had called for it. He felt once more that sharp stab of query. *Was* he a self-willed man without knowing it?

The tide of song swept him, thrilling him with its greatness, and bringing a strange wistfulness that he might have been a part of all this from its inception. Then with his newly awakened senses, he questioned keenly, was that pang he felt jealousy? He put that aside to think about later, for a man with a marvelous voice was singing a solo, not merely showing off his glorious voice, but singing a message to souls:

Not I, but Christ, be honored, loved, exalted;
Not I, but Christ, be seen, be known, be heard;
Not I, but Christ, in every look and action,
Not I, but Christ, in every thought and word.

Christ, only Christ, no idol ever falling;
Christ, only Christ, no needless bustling sound;
Christ, only Christ, no self-important bearing;
Christ, only Christ, no trace of "I" be found.

O to be saved from myself, dear Lord,
O to be lost in Thee,
O that it might be no more I,
But Christ, that lives in me.

The words sank deep into his soul, and added to his discomfort. Up there in the shadows of the vaulted ceiling, somewhere above the gallery, he seemed to feel a Presence whose eyes were searching him through and through!

But the voice of the preacher broke in upon his thoughts. It was the Dr. Leveridge whom Harry Sharpless and Lawyer Harris had met so eagerly on the train! Frank looked up, prejudiced against him already, and studied the kind, strong face, the fine head crowned with silver hair, the keen eyes. But in spite of his prejudice he could not but admire the cultured voice of the speaker as he announced his text:

"If we have forgotten the name of our God, or stretched out our hands to a strange god; shall not God search this out? for he knoweth the secrets of the heart."

The verse was utterly unfamiliar to Frank Brandon and startled him as if the words had been spoken for him alone. It reached even to joints and marrow and divided the very soul and spirit of him. It seemed to Frank Brandon that he had never heard a verse of Scripture before that so searched his being. He wondered in his astonishment where the preacher had found such a verse. He did not remember having heard it before. Some new translation, probably! But it gave him for the first time in his life the consciousness of God searching out his innermost secrets. God right there looking into his thoughts! A great panic swept over him, causing him to doubt whether God would really find everything in him entirely satisfactory. Was he, after all, quite as letter-perfect as he had always supposed himself? This sudden amazing jolt to his usually complacent spirit, added to the discomfort of his body, made his situation almost unbearable. He indignantly put away such thoughts and set his lips to smile approbation. His whole attitude and expression ought to show keen interest and enjoyment. He must carry this through to the end at all odds.

The preacher swept on with a discourse that burned into his soul with a new kind of torture. He began by speaking of things that go toward making a soul forget God. Prominent in the list, he mentioned great Christian activity, especially the kind in which men make a plan and ask God to bless it, rather than waiting on the Lord to discover what he would have done. He tore the halo from the Christian who is immersed in this sort of man-planned activity by holding up to view a Lord whose very love constrains the heart to look to him and "lean not to its own understanding."

Frank Brandon listened in amazement to a doctrine he had never heard even hinted at before. He knew in his honest heart that nearly everything that he had ever done in the name of Christ had been after this sort, and if this were true he was being condemned. He tried to reason against it all, to protest in his soul, but the preacher was backing up every word he said with a verse of Scripture.

Then the preacher went on to speak of strange gods that men commonly set up in their souls. Money, pleasure, worldly amusement, fleshly lust—

Ah! Frank lifted up his head triumphantly. None of these were enshrined in his heart. Of that he was very sure. He had lived a clean life, he had no time for worldly amusement, or personal pleasure, and he was not especially fond of money. Look how well he had behaved that morning when the bank closed! He had always given largely of what he possessed. He did not feel condemned in any of those ways.

But now the speaker had come to another god, the commonest one, he said, the one most often enshrined in the human heart. That was Self. Self-will, self-esteem, having one's own way, the desire to dominate, even over God himself, and bend his way to our will.

He went into the matter most fully and keenly. Like a surgeon using the scalpel of the Word of God, he laid bare Frank Brandon's true self to his own eyes. He saw himself by his very activities putting God out and himself in, getting praise to himself instead of God; actually singing praises to himself. That heathenish little verse flashed through his harried mind.

I love me! I love me!
I'm wild about myself!

He began to see that his very attendance tonight at this strange meeting had been for the worship of self, an attempt to put self back on its pedestal before the world.

In closing the speaker brought out the fact that this self-worship was the sin of Satan who once was Lucifer, son of the morning, the anointed cherub, until iniquity was found in him. Satan's sin was in trying to put himself in God's place. The speaker quoted the awful condemnation:

How art thou fallen from heaven, O Lucifer, son of the morning! how art thou cut down to the ground, which didst weaken the nations!

For thou hast said in thine heart, I will ascend into heaven, I will exalt my throne above the stars of God: I will sit also upon the mount of the congregation, in the sides of the north:

I will ascend above the heights of the clouds; I will be like the most High.

Yet thou shalt be brought down to hell, to the sides of the pit!

From then on Frank Brandon was engrossed in his task of heart-searching until they began to sing in closing that hymn of consecration:

Have thine own way, Lord! Have thine own way!
Thou art the Potter, I am the clay.
Mold me and make me after thy will,
While I am waiting yielded and still.

He knew those words. He had taught them to many an audience. He had always urged them not to drag. "Make it snappy!" he used to say. Never before had the words meant a thing to him. Now they thrilled through him like an alien prayer in which his lips were forced to join, but his soul was full of wild rebellion, struggling to keep self on its shrine.

He did the proper thing at the close of the meeting: shook hands with the preacher and those active in the conference; told them how sorry he was that his other dates had prohibited his being present at every session, said how wonderful the meeting had been, and how much he knew he had missed; told them to count on him for anything he could do to keep up the spirit of the conference; explained how he was president of this, chairman of that, leader of the other, his time so filled that he could scarcely ever do anything extra. And then suddenly he realized that nobody was listening to him. Nobody seemed to have noticed his absence nor to be especially delighted that he was here tonight. They seemed to take it for granted that anybody would be there who could!

Finally, with a sick sense that he could not stand much more and ought to be in bed, he found Emily behind her post and hurried home.

Sometime in the night he awoke to the knowledge that he was very ill indeed. His body was on fire with fever and yet shivering with cold. His eyes were burning, his head was throbbing, his limbs aching unbearably, and his throat swollen almost shut.

Emily was up doing things for him, asking him wearisome questions that he did not want to answer. There were hot-water bags about him and an ice bag on his head. A doctor was there somewhere in the dimness of things. Was that possibly a nurse in the

offing? And Emily beside the bed on her knees sobbing—it might even be praying.

It all wearied him inexpressibly and he wandered
off into a strange place of fire and ice. He did not
want to go but it seemed some duty was compelling
him; and then he saw before him shrines, his and
Emily's. They were like two wooden alcoves on the
clear icy pavement, with shelves above a kneeling
place, and pictures in costly frames upon the shelves,
and haloes over the pictures. He stepped closer to
see the picture in his own shrine and found it was a
likeness of himself! He was startled to notice what a
proud and haughty expression he wore, hard, worldly! Was he like that? And did God search it out and
see it? He looked again and now he saw there was sin
in his face. Actual sin!

Heartsick, he stepped aside to see what picture
was in Emily's shrine, and lo, it was not her own likeness that was there, but another picture of his own
haughty self with a self-satisfied smile upon his face.
He wondered in his fevered brain whether in the
eyes of God it was any better for a woman to have
her husband in God's place rather than herself? He
dimly perceived that they were both strange gods in
the eyes of God. Then somehow there seemed to be
a compelling force upon him that made it necessary
for him to go back to his own shrine and worship.
Pray to himself! How could he?

Ah, there were prayers stored up upon the shelf—
many of them! High-sounding words full of fleshly
desires, ending always: "Bless *my*self, *my* work,

make all *my* schemes succeed and *my* enemies fail."
They seemed so empty now as he took them down
and read them over painfully upon his knees.

And now a song of praise to his strange god was
required of him, and there was only one song he
knew. His voice suddenly shrilled out through the
sick room, startling the nurse and Emily as they
hovered anxiously near at hand. It wasn't the voice
wherewith he had charmed audiences with wonderful solos, nor yet the rich tones wherewith he had
carried audiences into great tides of song. It was a
high, excited, fevered voice shrilling and breaking
and fading into nothing.

I love me! I love me!
  I'm wild about myself!

"Oh Frank! *Don't! Please* don't!" sobbed Emily,
very far away.

"But I *must*, Emily," he protested petulantly.
"Don't you see the picture there on my shelf? I *have*
to sing."

I love me! I love me!
  There's my picture-on-my-shelf!

His voice suddenly trailed away into silence.

Then he looked up at the picture and saw an
astonishing thing. For now the picture, though himself unmistakably, nevertheless had the evil, handsome eyes of Lucifer, son of the morning, and he
saw even out of the murk of his delirium that "whoso
putteth himself in the place of God" is really putting
there Satan, the tempter of the world, the enemy of

God, the enemy of the Savior of the world. And suddenly Frank Brandon knew himself to be a sinner and cried aloud in awful anguish!

"Oh *God!* Forgive! Help! *Help!*"

The nurse thought that he was in pain and gave him a soothing powder till he slept.

But Emily upon her knees beside the bed was praying! She thought that he was dying, and she prayed, *really* prayed, perhaps for the first time in her life.

A long time afterward he awoke in the dim quiet of the sick room. Emily and the nurse were hovering in silence not far away, awaiting the outcome.

Suddenly the hush of the room was broken once more by song.

It was still not the voice with which he used to charm audiences or conduct choruses so successfully. It was not even the voice with which he had sung that strange grotesque melody when he was taken sick, or the voice with which he had cried out to God for mercy when he saw himself and his own sin. It was a thin, high thread of a voice, burned out with fever, and quavering with weakness.

Oh—to—be—saved from myself—*dear Lord!*
  Oh—to—be—lost in Thee!
Oh—that it might be—no—more—*I,*
  But Christ—*that lives—in—me!*

At the first breath Emily crept to his side and knelt, slipping her hand into the thin white hand that lay so feebly on the coverlet. But the feeble fingers held her own in a weak pressure, and the shadow of a smile trembled over his lips as he said faintly, pausing for breath:

"Isn't that what we want it to be, dear—from—now—on? *Christ—in—us?*"

"Oh, yes," she answered softly, "just his will! Frank, dearest, do you know, it was not until I handed you over to him, and prayed, 'Not my will, but thine be done,' that he gave you back to me, and you began to get better."

It was very quiet in the room, while a soft understanding passed from one hand to the other, and then tenderly two voices instead of one quavered out into the silence again.

Have thine own way, Lord, have thine own way!
Hold o'er my being absolute sway!
Fill with thy Spirit till all shall see
Christ only, always, living in me!

The nurse was standing just outside the door listening to see if she would be needed, and now she turned away with a strange mistiness in her eyes, saying softly to herself:

"Well, those two must have been real, after all! I didn't think they were!"

THE LOST
MESSAGE

*T*HE Rev. John Tresevant sat in his well-appointed study on Saturday morning at nine-thirty, trying to bring his mind down to writing a sermon for the next day.

He had just returned from his vacation, a cruise on the luxurious yacht of a wealthy parishioner, Elliot Rand. He had expected to come back not only renewed in physical energy, but with his mind full of new, vigorous ideas for sermons and full preparation for at least two Sundays ahead.

But he had not found the atmosphere of the yacht conducive to thought or work. There had been many lively guests on board, and he was expected to enter into all the gaiety of the lazy days, on a smooth sea under a blue sky. The moonlit nights were spent in the company of people who neither knew nor cared anything about theology. Also the cruise had been prolonged four days beyond the original time planned, so that this was the very last day before the minister's vacation ended. And he had nothing prepared for the morrow. It was imperative that he work hard all day, and he never felt less like work.

The telephone did its part in hindering. It rang incessantly. Mrs. Brown had broken her leg, and longed to see her pastor. She was the wife of another prominent member of his session. Her wishes were law. Mr. Addison was in the hospital with pneumonia and not expected to live from hour to hour. Mrs. Addison was the president of the Ladies' Aid, and most efficient, and she had been telephoning for three days for attendance from her pastor. Old Mrs. Hargraves was dead and the funeral must be arranged for, the family visited. Mrs. Barker had just been taken to the insane asylum and her husband had asked that the pastor call as soon as possible.

He was beginning to get desperate. He had started just one sentence on the smooth, expensive paper that lay before him, and he wasn't quite sure whether he was pleased with it or not.

Again the telephone rang.

He turned his annoyed glance toward the innocent little black instrument of torture and reached out his hand to the receiver.

"Yes?"

That tone of his was perfect. It could easily rise into wrath or soothe into honeyed tones, according to the status of the intruder. Much practice had made it a marvel of its kind.

And then it was only his wife, Elaine! Elaine, who knew just what he had to do, and what interruptions meant to him, to be so thoughtless as to call him from the country club where he knew she had gone that morning to play golf! It was too annoying!

"My *dear!*" His tone indicated that she was anything but dear at that moment.

"Now, you needn't get cross, John," said Elaine's honeyed tones. "I'm not calling on my own initiative. It's Elliot Rand who wants you. He has some people here; he wants to have them meet you. They have slews of money and they are just looking for a place to put it. He says they would just as soon as not put it into some marvelous stained glass windows for our new church if they happen to like you. He wants you to come down at once and play in a foursome with them. I'm taking the women to lunch at the club, and you've simply *got* to come!"

"But—my *dear!*" The tone was accusatory. "My sermons—!"

"Yes, I told him, John, that you had to work. I made it as strong as I could, but he said this was more important than any sermons, and that it didn't matter what you preached, you could just preach some old sermon over again and the people would never know! He said anyway that you simply *must* come!"

"I don't see how I possibly can—" began John Tresevant. "Mrs. Hargraves is dead and Mr. Addison may be dying of pneumonia—"

"Well, you can't bring Mrs. Hargraves to life, nor keep Mr. Addison from dying," said Elaine in a sweet, irresponsible voice, "and Elliot Rand *wants* you, so you know what you have to do! Put on your white flannel suit. It's in your closet. The tailor just brought it back this morning. I'll tell Jasper to get out your golf clubs and have them ready, and I'll drive back and get you. Hurry. They want to start playing at once! Wear that blue tie I bought you, the one that matches your eyes, you know. It's in the upper drawer of your chiffonier."

In the end, of course, he went. He had known from the first that he would have to. He hung up with a despairing look at that one sentence, not yet completed: "The trouble with the world today is—"

Would it be possible for him to do some thinking about his theme while he was playing golf? What was his theme, anyway, and was there a text that would be apt in connection with this thought?

While he hastily put on the white flannels and the blue tie according to instructions, he was threshing his brains and trying to get an inspiration. Surely, surely his fertile brain would not play him false. He had of late gained great confidence in himself. If worse came to worst he could surely extemporize— just look up three or four good illustrations and build something around them. He had always been a ready speaker. But that was not what he had wanted to do that first Sunday after his return from vacation. He had wanted to preach something that would impress not only the church, but the public press, the city of admirers and adherents. He had made a reputation for wise sayings, and deep intellectual addresses that were called "profound," and "challenging," and "epoch-revealing" according to the degree of education and imagination of the various press reporters, and he wanted to keep it up. Especially at the start of a new season, he wanted to do something really brilliant, and to do him justice he was filled with panic to think how little time he had in which to achieve this great end.

If he went to the country club he couldn't hope to get away until afternoon at best. And yet, as Elaine had stated, it was Elliot Rand who had asked it, so he must go. Elliot Rand simply owned the church. Whatever he wanted must be done, or the flow of money would stop. Elliot Rand had ways of looking coldly at anyone who dared to differ from him in the slightest degree. Elliot Rand had to be pleased at any cost.

The day was deliriously lovely, and the golf course perfect. The Mr. Clinton whom Elliot Rand desired to please out of some money for stained glass windows was a crack player, and a most interesting personality, and so was his cousin, a professor in a great eastern university. John Tresevant, as he placed his ball and took his stance, had a feeling that he had a mental reprieve, and might enjoy himself at least for the morning. After lunch he certainly must excuse himself and make those calls briefly, and then lock himself into his study and get to work.

But after lunch the rest of the foursome were keen for another eighteen holes. They liked the handsome young preacher with his sure strokes and his witty tongue. Tresevent said he really must go, and described the distresses of his various parishioners briefly. But Elliot Rand gave him a look that flung all his excuses to the winds. He mimicked each of the poor and distressed most laughably, and practically required his presence for the afternoon.

"It is most important, my dear fellow!" he said in a low tone with a persuasive hand on Tresevant's arm, and a look that made it quite impossible to get away.

The sun was beginning to send long slant rays across the smooth greens, when John Tresevant, triumphant, with an enviably low score, and fresh from a swim in the pool and a shower, met the ladies of the party who had been having their own game of bridge on the wide veranda of the club house. He intended to partake of the delicious lemonade and then hurry away to his belated work.

"And now, Tresevant," said Elliot Rand cheerfully as they settled down in the comfortable rockers to sip their cold drink, "we've decided to make a day of it and all drive up the mountain and have dinner together. You needn't begin to make excuses again. I have it all fixed up. You see you are known to have gone away with me for your vacation, and not a half dozen of the flock will realize that you are home. Your vacation doesn't end anyway until midnight tonight and I intend personally to see that you get every fraction of a second of the time. Besides, my friend Clinton here wants to talk something over with you. He has an idea about those windows if he decides to arrange for it, and it is really imperative that you tell him your wishes concerning coloring and subjects, you know. I tried to sketch your plan to him, but I couldn't remember everything you said, and I want you to talk with him. We're bringing him back for the midnight train, and there won't be any other time, as he's sailing for Europe next week."

"Why, I could send you over the list of subjects," said the young minister politely, "but I really don't see how I could possibly spare the evening. I have no preparation for tomorrow—"

"That's all right, Tresevant," said Elliot Rand with a laughing wave of the hand, "we'll excuse you from being intellectual tomorrow. No preacher tries to do much in the pulpit the first Sunday after his vacation. And you know there won't be anybody out that matters anyway. They haven't come back from their vacations yet."

Tresevant drew his brows as he sipped his drink, and tried to puzzle it out. How was he going to do all that was required of him and yet take in this new delightful interlude?

And even as he thought, his host was again planning his way for him, as he had been doing for the past two weeks, just a downy bed of ease to rest his luxurious soul upon.

"He has plenty of old sermons, hasn't he, Mrs. Tresevant?" Elliot Rand was saying to Elaine.

"Why, of course!" she acquiesced. "They're all over the place and he won't let me clear them up and put them away. And just the day before we went away there arrived a whole big cabinet full of his earlier sermons. I'm sure he hasn't ever tried them on this church at all, for they've been stored at his father's house in New England."

"There!" cried Elliot Rand, "that settles it! We

won't take no for an answer. Seriously, Tresevant, I ask this as a special favor!"

Elliot Rand fixed his fine eyes on the minister's face and smiled one of those cocksure smiles. Tresevant knew he must give in, or break with this man who took it so for granted that he owned him; and such a break would be a more serious matter than he was prepared to make on so short a notice.

Suddenly Tresevant put down his half-finished glass on the table beside him and rose to his feet.

"That being the case," he said gravely, almost haughtily, "I shall have to leave you at once and go to the hospital before I can possibly go anywhere else. I promised Mrs. Addison—"

"Oh—is Addison one of those on your list? Well, of course, you could stop there on the way. It ought not to take you long. He may not even be living. They told me this morning he hadn't a chance."

"You knew that this morning?" asked the minister with a startled look at his host. Then he turned quickly and started down the steps toward the hospital not far away. There were times when John Tresevant could be very decisive indeed, and now it had suddenly come over him what it would mean if this prominent man in his church should die without his attendance, and it should be found out that he had been playing golf nearby all day!

"We'll pick you up in ten minutes!" shouted Rand.

"Poor John! He's always so conscientious!" sighed Elaine prettily.

The men watched him thoughtfully.

"A most interesting man, your husband, Mrs.

Tresevant," observed the elder Mr. Clinton, the one with the money to invest for eternity.

Fifteen minutes later two cars drew up in front of the hospital and waited ten minutes more before the minister came down with a troubled look.

"I think you'll have to count me out!" he said decisively to Elliot Rand. "There are several other people I ought to see, and I really should get back to my study."

"Nonsense!" said that demogogue sharply. "Get in! We've waited long enough! Did you find Mr. Addison still living?"

"Yes, but unconscious. He is very near the end. I was there in time to offer a prayer. I think his wife would never have forgiven me if he had passed on without it, and—" he added thoughtfully, "I'm afraid I should never have forgiven myself."

"Oh, for pity's sake, John! How silly! What possible good could a prayer do, even if the man was conscious to hear it?" said Elaine contemptuously.

"Get in," said Elliot Rand again, this time with authority. "If you have to go anywhere else this evening, we're taking you, and making sure of you."

He held the door open for the minister and Tresevant got hesitantly into the car.

"I must go to Hargraves' to see about the funeral," he said, "and I must see Mr. Barker. His wife has been taken to the asylum and he wants me; and I should go to Mrs. Brown!"

"Nonsense!" said Elliot Rand sternly. "The Hargraves funeral can be arranged in the morning. You can telephone from the Mountain House that you expect to arrive home about midnight and will be over the first thing in the morning. As for Mr. Barker, there's no rush about him. I've known him a good many years and this isn't the first time his wife has been taken to the asylum. And Mrs. Brown has a broken leg and can't get up and leave the church to-night, so you are safe. You'll find your call just as acceptable tomorrow afternoon. No, forget it, parson, and let's have a good time. We've got you, and we mean to keep you!"

But John Tresevant sat unsmiling in his seat, looking troubled. It was not only that he had just been in the hovering presence of death. It was not wholly that he knew the prayer he had just uttered was nothing but empty words, hurrying to be fin-ished before the soul passed out of this world, that he might not be counted to have failed in his duty toward this prominent man. It was that he felt shamed. All day he had been racing after a good time to please others, with his conscience prodding him and reminding him that it was all wrong, the kind of life he was living.

As he settled back in the luxurious car and was rushed through the city and out into the far reaches of lovely country road, by clear winding rivers and towering rocks, through picturesque villages, with the hazy blue of a distant mountain for a goal, and a spirit of gaiety around him, somehow he seemed to be set apart from his companions. No longer could he forget his duty, and the oncoming services, for which he was not prepared, and enter into the good cheer of the hour. He was distraught and silent,

tired and worried. He realized that he would have
to sit up all night to get ready for his morning's
sermon. He must somehow think out a theme, with
an outline. That was the trouble with having set the
standard of fine preaching in the past. He must keep
it up. He could not have them saying that he was not
preaching as interesting sermons as formerly.

Elliot Rand might tell him that it didn't matter
what he preached, but he would not hesitate to criticize afterward. Tresevant knew by sorry experience.

But there was little time to meditate on sermons.
He was seated next to Mr. Clinton who began a
rapid fire of questions about the new church.

Then they were at the beautiful hotel before they
realized and spent a long time over the excellent
dinner that was served to them.

But at last it was time to start home. They chose
a different way to return because it was supposed to
be shorter and the hour was late.

They sped over the road at a good pace, until suddenly they came to a halt so abruptly that it almost
threw the whole company upon their knees. The car
behind belonging to the young professor barely
swerved in time to avoid a dangerous collision.

The road ahead was partly shut off and marked
with red lanterns. A sign announced that travelers
would proceed at their own risk, as the road was
under repair.

The men of the party got out and consulted, even
walking down the road under question for some distance. They finally decided to risk it, as they had

come more than halfway. They could not possibly get Mr. Clinton to his train if they went back by the other road, for there was no cross cut to it.

But the road grew worse and worse. In places it was corrugated and sent the travelers up in the air and down again with uneven rhythm, like a gigantic rocking horse. They groaned and laughed about it at first, but when this continued for several miles they grew silent and cross. There were no signs anywhere, and the moon had withdrawn behind an ominous cloud.

Then suddenly the leading car lurched and reeled, there was a grinding sound, and they came to a standstill at a fearful angle, with two of the wheels down in a gully of soft thick mud.

The men got out again to investigate, shaking their heads gravely. Then each with a desperate look at his shoes and his good clothes, stepped down into what seemed a fathomless abyss, and pitted his strength against the mammoth bulk of machinery that lolled in the muck and darkness. Tresevant was no shirker, and before many minutes his white flannels which had remained immaculate during the long, delightful day, were smeared beyond recognition with mud and grease.

Desisting at last from the impossible task of straightening up the car, Tresevant and the professor decided to walk up the mountain after assistance.

But it was hours later that a sadder and a wiser company of holiday makers were finally dragged up the mountain to a service station for repairs.

The minister grimly stood in the shadows at the side of the road and stared into the darkness while they waited for repairs. He was too weary to think, but he *must* decide what to do about a sermon.

The morning was about to dawn when at last the two cars got underway and started back to the road they had driven up so happily that afternoon.

They dropped the minister at his own door just as the milkman was going his morning rounds. But scarcely had Tresevant put the key in the lock of his front door before a car whirled up to the curb, and the Addison chauffeur came hurrying up the walk.

"Mr. Tresevant," he said respectfully, "Mrs. Addison says will you come right over to the hospital at once! Mr. Addison has rallied and is asking for you."

Tresevant looked down at his shoes and his smudged white flannels in dismay, yet he knew he must go.

"Oh, *John!* You must have some breakfast first!" said Elaine firmly.

"I was told to say that Mr. Addison may pass away at any moment, ma'am!" said the chauffeur, and there was almost contempt in the look he gave her.

"I'll be right with you," said Tresevant, tearing up the stairs three steps to a stride.

He climbed out of the soiled white flannels and muddy shoes and into his serge suit with a single movement as it were, made the gesture of washing his face, and combed his hair with a pocket comb on the way downstairs.

"John! You *mustn't!* You really *mustn't!*" called Elaine futilely.

Mr. Addison died a half-hour later, but Tresevant had gone through the form of another prayer with him, and Mrs. Addison was duly grateful. The Addison car delivered him at the manse again just as Elaine was coming down to breakfast. But the minister hadn't had time even to taste his coffee before the telephone rang.

"It's the Hargraves, sir," said the maid. "They say they must wire the married son about the funeral, and could you come over at once?"

Tresevant gulped a few swallows of coffee and went out again, amid more protests from Elaine, who had much to say about the trials of a minister's *wife*.

It was almost half past ten when the minister got back from Hargraves' and there was no sermon as yet!

Tresevant tore into his study and began to fling neat manuscripts about wildly. There on his desk lay his effort of yesterday morning smiling up at him in clear fair script: "The trouble with the world today is—"

If he could only get hold of the thread of his theme! But to save him all he could think of that the world needed just now was some sleep.

Elaine was standing in the doorway smiling at him, fresh as a rose in her lovely fall costume.

"Where is that case of sermons you said came from home?" he yelled fiercely.

"Right over there in the corner, dearest!" she said sweetly. "But they're not open. You couldn't possibly get them open now. And you must go and put on a clean shirt and a necktie! Why, John! That's your old suit you have on! You'll *have* to change! And there! The second bell is ringing! Why not just give them a little talk about that lovely sunset we saw at sea last week. You can do it wonderfully, you know."

"Where is the axe? I ask you? Where is the axe, or a hatchet? Or even a hammer and screwdriver? Isn't there a tool of any sort around the house *ever?*" His tone was rising far above the ordinary ministerial modulation, and the maid appeared at the door with the axe.

The minister grasped it and went for the sermon case as though it were an enemy threatening the life of his family. *Crash!* came down the axe on the stubborn wood. *Crash!*

"John! What will the people going by think at hearing such sounds from the manse on Sunday morning?"

Crash!

"I don't care what they think!" said the minister.

"John! You will ruin that lovely mahogany cabinet inside. Why will you be so silly? You can't possibly hunt a sermon now. John! I only sent for that because I wanted that lovely cabinet for my music, and now you're ruining it!"

Crash!

"I'll be ruined myself if I can't find a sermon," said the minister, bringing down his axe ruthlessly and splintering the outer box with fervor.

Another crash or two and the box was conquered,

and simultaneously the cabinet door sprang open, letting out an avalanche of manuscripts in neat brown paper covers.

The minister pounced upon one almost gleefully. It looked familiar and gave him comfort. At least it was *some*thing. If it didn't suit the high and mighty Elliot Rand it was his own fault, and he would tell him so when he came around to criticize.

With a deep drawn breath, something like a sigh of relief, the minister caressed the sermon, and turned wildly toward the door, as the last stroke of the second bell sounded melodiously on the air.

"John! You're *not* going to church that way! You've got a smudge on your nose, and your hair looks like a haystack!" screamed his wife as he tore out the manse door and across the lawn to the church.

But John Tresevant strode on.

In the church study the elders were gathering for the formality of a prayer before the service, a ceremony instituted by a former pastor and insisted upon by an old-fashioned senior elder.

Tresevant knelt beside his chair and signed to the senior elder to pray. He reflected that he would have time to glance at the heading of his sermon during the singing, and find out what Scripture would be appropriate to read for it. He had always been so particular about writing down those little details when he first began his ministry.

"Lord, we pray thee that thou wilt be with our beloved pastor today and endue him with power from on high! *Help him*, Lord, that we may through his message behold Jesus, our Savior!"

The words were so typical of the senior elder that at any other time they would have passed the minister's preoccupied mind unaware, but suddenly they took life and rang in his ears. Help! That was what he needed! Help! How he used to cry to God for help in those early days. How uncertain he used to be of himself, and how dependent upon God! How he *used* to get almost in a panic before he went into the pulpit, lest he would fail, and bring dishonor upon his Lord! He almost smiled as he remembered. For now he was so certain of himself—usually. He used to say that he must spend as much time in prayer as he spent in study or his message was a failure. Now his prayers were wild and hurried and desultory, with his mind upon the unique and arresting sentences with which his discourse was to open.

Suddenly he realized that he was in a worse panic now than he had ever been in his life before. His brain was empty and his mind was in a whirl. He had nothing, absolutely nothing, between him and disaster but that little brown-paper-covered sermon in his hand.

"God! Help me! Give me a message! God! God! Where are you? Can't you hear me anymore?"

It was all in his heart, this wild cry. The senior elder had brought his prayer to a close and given place to the one next in authority, a little man with a thin, unconvincing voice who was droning out a list of requests.

But Tresevant did not hear them. Suddenly it was the Lord Himself who was standing there in his study, looking down upon him. He could feel His hand laid upon his head, and His voice was as clear in his heart as words spoken.

"John Tresevant," he said, "you and I used to walk together. Do you remember that? You and I died together on the cross years ago. Have you forgotten that? In those days when we walked together I could give you my messages, and you could carry them to souls that needed them, but you have walked strange paths of late, paths where I could not go, and you have been so far away from me that you could not hear my voice. Even when you asked for help you did not come near enough to get it. You are too far away this morning. You do not really want my help. You think you are smart enough to do this thing yourself, so you will have to do it alone. I cannot help you till you are ready to walk with me again, and can hear my voice. You will have to do the best you can!"

The prayers around the minister suddenly ceased. He mumbled a few words of formal closing and arose, his face white and drawn, and went unsmiling, unseeing, into his pulpit, the little old brown-paper-covered sermon clutched in his hand, the only connection between himself and a deserted God.

He found the place in the Bible, the Scripture he was to read, but he was suddenly faced with the realization that next in order was the long prayer, and praying meant addressing the God who had just spoken to his heart back there in the study, who had rebuked him for not walking with Him! And what could he say to a God who had separated Himself from him?

Down there in the audience sat Elliot Rand, with Mr. Clinton and the professor. Yesterday Elliot Rand had laughingly boasted about what wonderful prayers his minister made, comparing them to a beautiful embroidery of words. That was what was expected of him now, to embroider a prayer for the delicate ears of his congregation, a prayer that should be a fitting accompaniment to, and perhaps suggest, the mellow light of costly windows in a new edifice. And suddenly John Tresevant was afraid of God, the God whom he, as the mouthpiece of a large audience, must approach in prayer.

Back in the early days of his ministry, when his heart was on fire for God, when his whole being was filled with a zeal for soul-winning, and his consciousness was always permeated with the sense of the presence of God, his prayers vibrated with love. Praying had been like coming to a loving Father, knowing that what he asked would be granted because he and his Father were of one accord. It flashed upon him now that he had lost this close fellowship with God, that the prayer he was about to make was a counterfeit, a mere display of words.

He opened his lips to speak and the Lord stood there before him, looking into his soul again with that searching gaze. The Lord, with his pierced hands and his wounded side and the look of hurt love in his eyes. And suddenly Tresevant's flow of gracious words was cut off, and he had nothing wherewith to cry out to God but the humble, contemptible confessions of a sinner!

He forgot to pray for "the president and officers of these United States," and "for those in authority." He forgot to pray for those on foreign fields carrying the message, forgot the sick and suffering, the sad and fearful, and prayed only for mercy! And yet such was the sincerity of his prayer that somehow every man, woman, and child in the audience was made to feel his own need of mercy, and that the prayer was especially for him.

It was very still in the room while he was praying, and when the petition was ended more than one in the audience was wiping his eyes.

But Tresevant was not watching his audience. He was conscious only of that Presence that was standing in his pulpit with him. The Presence that during the first two years of his ministry had been with him always when he preached. Then his message had been given to please his Lord and not his congregation.

Where had that Presence been? Why had he lost the sense of his nearness? *When* had he lost it? He tried to think back. Did it begin about the time when he first met Elaine, the lovely girl who had seemed so far above him socially, financially, and yet so desirable, so angelic? Had he wandered away from the Lord to please Elaine? And now to please his congregation? Elliot Rand?

These thoughts like accusing persons seemed to flock around him and hide his congregation from his view, as he sat down in the great pulpit chair and shaded his eyes with his hand while the costly organ swelled forth the hymn, and the people, led by the well-trained choir, sang.

Tresevant did not hear his congregation singing.

"God," he was saying behind his sheltering hand, "O God, I can't do it. I'm going to break down. I've never broken down, but now I'm done. You'll have to help me. My strength and my assurance are gone!"

Elaine watched him with startled, annoyed eyes as he rose with white stricken face to read the Scripture. So silly for him to think he had to go out to those clamoring parishioners when he so needed sleep!

It was the thirty-eighth Psalm that the sermon had called for, and suddenly as he glanced at its heading Tresevant recalled it and it seemed the very cry of his own soul. Unconsciously he read aloud the notes he had carefully printed in the margin of his Bible, put there long ago when the great truths first gripped him.

" 'This Psalm is the cry of a saved soul under conviction of sin.' Its heading in our Bibles reads: A psalm of David, *to bring to remembrance!* It reminds us of Paul's words in the New Testament: 'If we would judge ourselves we would not be judged!' "

The minister paused as the crushing truths broke upon his own soul. The congregation was breathless. Then slowly he read, as if he had forgotten the people, as if he were crying out himself to that Presence there before him in the pulpit.

"O Lord, rebuke me not in thy wrath; neither chasten me in thy hot displeasure. There is no soundness in my flesh because of thine anger; neither is there any rest in my bones because of my sin. For mine iniquities are gone over my head; as a heavy burden they are too heavy for me—" his voice broke and he brought out his confession clearly, "because of—my—*foolishness!*"

A sob almost broke through the huskiness of the minister's voice. The audience was tensely still. Elliot Rand was listening in horrified, incredulous contempt, but the man standing before his God neither saw nor cared.

On he read through the verses that followed, even reading aloud his interpolated notes.

" 'Lord . . . my groaning is not hid from thee . . .'—the cry of a soul in anguish. 'In thee, O Lord, do I hope . . .' Confession of sin at last: 'For I will declare my iniquity; I will be sorry for my sin. . . . Forsake me not, O Lord. O my God be not far from me. Make haste to help me, O Lord my salvation.' "

As Tresevant finished reading and sat down, the hush was instantly filled with soft organ tones and the choir broke forth into lovely music as if to soothe the minds so strangely stirred, and cause them to forget the ugly words about *sin*.

Tresevant was clutching that sermon that he must now preach. In the light of that chapter he had just read he must get up and preach!

And now he knew which sermon this was that he held in his hand. It was one that had been written almost upon his knees, and it had never been delivered except after much prayer. He had always gone to deliver it as to a sacred trust, gone with his face shining from communion with his Lord. And that sermon had always brought fruit for Christ.

But that was a long time ago, when he walked with his God. That was before he knew Elaine, or Elliot Rand; when he had a plain little church with a congregation that was hungry for the word of truth.

Now he was standing in a worldly congregation where he had many times smothered the truth in pretty phrases. Now his sin of estrangement had come between his Lord and himself and it seemed to him that the message was no longer his to give.

He arose and stood staring down at the words. It was then that he suddenly realized that the opening sentence of this sermon was identical with the one he had started on Saturday morning:

"The trouble with the world today is—"

Of course he hadn't been able to finish it then. He hadn't known then what was the trouble with the world. *Now* he knew!

"The trouble with the world today is that it has lost its sense of sin, and of its awful need of a Savior!"

The startled congregation, already deeply stirred by the unusual prayer and Scripture reading, sat up and stared at him.

But Tresevant went on setting forth great truths, the old familiar sentences sweeping to his lips.

"Men today are unwilling to admit their sin because that would hurt their pride. It is a humbling thing to confess sin! Men are provoked when God discounts all of their self-righteousnesses and calls them filthy rags!"

Elliot Rand was beginning to get angry. Two red spots appeared on his cheeks. Was his prince of a preacher going fanatical on him?

Elaine stared at her husband contemptuously. Was this really John Tresevant daring to give voice to such outworn puritanical dogmas? What would people think?

But the people were weeping and listening breathlessly.

"Men are playing with life today," said Tresevant earnestly, "and God is waiting, watching, searching hearts! Looking with longing eyes at his redeemed ones, those of us who have named his name, and accepted him as our Savior, and have started out— to—witness—for him—"

Suddenly Tresevant paused, his voice broke, he bent his head an instant, drawing a deep breath. Then lifting his haggard face he tried once more to go on with husky broken voice, but the words halted upon his lips and he closed his eyes. Then looking up he said in a low tragic tone:

"I am not worthy. *I* have sinned! I cannot go on!"

He turned back to his pulpit chair and sank into it with his face in his hands.

There was an awful moment of silence during which it seemed that heaven and hell were awaiting the outcome, and God stood there in the pulpit with condemning eyes looking at them all.

Then suddenly a voice at the back of the church began to pray. It was the old senior elder whom nobody ever reckoned of any account.

"O our God, *all* we like sheep have gone astray,

we have turned every one to his own way, but thou hast laid upon thy Son the iniquity of us all. We thank thee for the Lord Jesus today, for we have seen *him*, hanging on the cross for us, bearing the cruel penalty of our sins, taking punishment by punishment all that was meant for us, all that was by right our score to settle. We have seen what he has done for us, and in the presence of his glory and his grace we have seen as in a mirror, our own silly, sinful selves, groveling here after the tinsel and toys put out by the enemy of our souls to decoy us from life and eternal joy with thee. O Lord, we thank thee for this vision of ourselves, and for the vision of thee we have had today. We have for a long time been longing for this, and we thank thee that today thou hast given to the earthly shepherd of our souls this message for us. So we confess our guilt and come to thee for cleansing—"

Suddenly there was a little stir in the center of the church and Elliot Rand, followed by the Clintons, stalked silently down the aisle and left the church. And Elaine with a frightened furtive glance at her husband, slipped out as silently as a shadow.

Then, as if the enemy had gone out like a troop, the Spirit of the Lord seemed suddenly to descend upon that gathering, as one after another of the members of the church took up the prayer of the old Scotch elder, till prayer had swept like a heavenly fire about that room. Prayer laden with confession of sin. Prayer for the pastor and for the church. Prayer for the town.

They lingered a long time afterward, asking forgiveness of one another, telling their pastor how he had searched their hearts, how they had been helped and blessed, shaking his hand with deep feeling, with tears, urging him to preach like that all the time, blessing the Lord for sending him.

But when at last John Tresevant went slowly out the door with the old Scotch elder by his side, he saw standing by the curb the luxurious limousine in which he had gone holidaying yesterday, and by it stood his wife and Elliot Rand talking most earnestly together.

They met him with strange, forced, alien smiles.

"Get in, Tresevant," said Elliot Rand kindly, as one might talk to a sick child. "We are taking you somewhere to rest."

The minister turned and looked at his erstwhile friend and host. There was a strange new light in his eyes that Elliot Rand did not know.

"To rest?" he said. "I don't need rest. I have just got back to the resting place of my soul!" and there was a new ring to his voice that Elliot Rand had never heard.

"Yes?" said Elliot Rand. "Well, get in, please. We are going to take you to a lovely place where your body may have rest, too. You needn't stop to explain to the congregation. I'll attend to all that. Just get in and lie back and rest. I feel that we owe you a great apology for keeping you on such a long strain all night."

There was a light in Tresevant's eyes as he faced Elliot Rand.

"Oh, *that?*" he said. "I'd forgotten about the night.

That was nothing! It is good of you of course to try to plan for me, but I haven't time now to go anywhere to rest. I've found my Lord and I intend never to leave him again. Tonight's service is coming, and I must find out what my Lord would have me do about it. Good-bye." And he turned and walked across the lawn to the manse.

"John!" cried his wife in dismay. But he did not seem to hear her.

A few minutes later she burst into his study, an angry spot of color on each cheek, and fire in her eyes.

"Well, just what do you think you are doing now?" she demanded as she entered. "Are you trying to make me ashamed that I ever married you, or have you lost your mind, or what? I never saw such an exhibition in all my life! A nice way to treat Elliot Rand after all he's done for you!"

And then she stopped, for she saw her husband was on his knees beside his desk praying.

He glanced up and there was such a look of radiance upon his face that she stepped back in a kind of awe. She had not seen that look on his face in a long, long time.

"MY BROTHER'S KEEPER"

*T*HREE young men sat together one Sunday afternoon in the reception room of a private boarding-house. The day was rainy and disagreeable, and at least two of the young men looked bored by the state of circumstances. They had read the morning paper through, yawned many times, and made all the remarks about the weather that they could think of. The third young man was a comparative stranger to the others. He was a young fellow with quiet manners and a frank, open face which commanded respect and invited friendship. Both Edward Burton and Charlie Stone felt a desire to know him better as they watched him seat himself by the window with his open book. That pleasant, firm mouth and those wisely merry eyes were interesting. They felt impelled to enter into conversation with him, and each searched his mind for a topic with which to begin. Edward Burton found it first, and began,

"Did you go out to see Bernhardt last evening, Murray?"

"No, I did not."

There seemed to be a quiet putting aside of the subject in the tone of this answer, and Edward was quick enough to see that he had started out on a wrong line; but Charlie was full of enthusiasm the minute the subject was mentioned.

"Oh, didn't you go? That's too bad. You missed it. But perhaps you were there the night before? It's the finest thing of the season."

The mild, quiet eyes were raised again; and the young man replied, "I never attend the theater."

There was none of the "I-am-better-than-thou" tone in this reply. Therefore the young men did not feel as if a bombshell had exploded in their midst, making it desirable to close up the conversation as soon as possible and get out of the room. They rather experienced a feeling of wonder, and perhaps of a sort of envy, at this young acquaintance who could so composedly say that he never took part in what was to them so intense a pleasure, and almost a constant temptation.

"Don't you ever go?" asked Edward. "I know many people do not approve of Bernhardt. I don't much myself. I just thought I'd go once. But there are good theaters, good, helpful plays, instructive, you know, and all that. Don't you go to any theaters?"

"No," was the pleasant answer. "I don't go to any."

"Well, I'm sure I wish you'd tell me why," said

Charlie. "Of course there are bad theaters, but I don't see what that has to do with the good ones. You might as well say you won't read any books at all because there are some bad ones written. That would cut you off from the Bible, don't you see? What's the difference? I've been to some theaters that did me a great deal of good. I have been to theaters all my life, and never got any harm from them that I could see. What's your theory, anyway?"

"My theory is this," answered the young man thus appealed to. "The theater, as an institution, is a bad thing. Its principal actors and actresses are people of known immoral character; the large majority of the plays enacted have at least objectional portions, which is putting it very mildly. If you don't believe that, study up the question and you'll find it so. I have a little book upstairs that you can read if you like. It is called 'Plain Talks About the Theater.' It is by Dr. Herrick Johnson, a man who knows what he is talking about; and it contains some of the most tremendous facts I have ever found. It makes this a solemn question."

"Well, but," said Charlie, who had evidently been waiting impatiently for a chance to speak, "what's that got to do with the good ones? I suppose there are bad ones, but I can't see why that should affect the good ones. I think they are all right. I can't see any harm in going to a theater when it's a good play."

"For one thing," answered young Murray quietly, "the same management that on one, or two, or three nights in the week places upon its stage what is commonly called a good play, the other nights in the week places there something which you could not in decency listen to or observe—"

"Stay away then," interrupted Charlie eagerly. "Don't you see, you'd only be patronizing the good ones, and showing the management that you would only uphold the good ones?" He finished with a triumphant flourish, as if he thought there was nothing left to be said.

"But," said the other, smiling, "your money goes to help along a management that is doing a business of death. What do you suppose it matters to them what you pay them your money for? They are willing you should choose Monday night instead of Tuesday. On Monday night they will take your money, and on Tuesday they will take the money of some poor soul who hasn't your moral sense, who has perhaps seen you enter the same building the evening before, and knowing you to be a Christian, thinks your example one to be followed; and it may be on Tuesday night there is something for him to see that will plant the seeds of eternal death in his soul."

"Oh, well," said Charlie carelessly, "I can't be looking out for everyone else. If I take care of myself and see that I do what is right, I think I'll be doing pretty well. If other people have a mind to go wrong, why, I can't help it."

"Can't you? Oughtn't you to help it?" said the other young man, lifting those quiet gray eyes to look searchingly at him. "What will you do when God asks you, as he asked Cain, 'Where is thy brother?' The Bible says that 'none of us liveth to himself, and no man dieth to himself,' and it tells us that 'we that

are strong ought to bear the infirmities of the weak,
and not to please ourselves,' and 'Let no man put a
stumblingblock or an occasion to fall in his brother's
way.' "

"My! You have them right at your tongue's end,
haven't you?" exclaimed Charlie admiringly.

But Edward's face was more serious.

"I never realized that there were so many verses
of that sort in the Bible. Do you really think it ought
to be taken so literally? Haven't the times changed
a great deal, and people's views grown broader? If
you reason in the way that you have done, that
would set up a pretty high standard. Why, we
couldn't do a thing without stopping to think
whether it was going to hurt someone!" he said.

"Yes," said the young man, "I suppose times have
changed some. We have theaters and dancing and
card-playing and Sunday observance, and a good
many other things of that sort to think about now,
instead of the question of eating meat that was
offered to idols; but I do not see how that changes
the principle. I suppose people's views are growing
broader; but I do not see why that gives us any right
to broaden the Bible rules. God himself said that the
road that led to death was broad, and that many
traveled in it; and that the way of life was narrow,
and there were few that found it. Keeping in mind
what word of his, it seems to me a dangerous thing
when we can look ahead of us and see the path
growing broad. You and I are supposed to be in the
'strait and narrow way,' I believe." As he said this
the look on his face was one of tender, brotherly

friendship that made his two companions feel that they were honored by his acquaintance, and that it was their privilege to stand on higher ground than that on which they had been living.

"As to the verses I quoted," he went on, after pausing a moment, "there are scores of them. Listen." And he drew from his inner pocket a small Bible, and turned over the leaves rapidly. " 'It is good neither to eat flesh, nor to drink wine, nor any thing whereby thy brother stumbleth, or is offended, or is made weak.' 'But take heed lest by any means this liberty of yours become a stumblingblock to them that are weak.... And through thy knowledge shall the weak brother perish for whom Christ died? But when ye sin so against the brethren, and wound their weak conscience, ye sin against Christ. Wherefore, if meat make my brother to offend, I will eat no flesh while the world standeth, lest I make my brother to offend.' "

Charlie gave a prolonged, sober whistle.

"That's putting it pretty strong, I must admit," he said. "You seem to know all about that book. Wish I knew as much. You ought to be a minister."

"I have been preaching quite a sermon, haven't I?" he said. "Well, you should not have started me off."

"Oh, don't stop!" said Edward. "I'm interested. I've been troubled about the theater sometimes myself. My father didn't approve of it; but he never told me his reasons, and I couldn't see that it ever did me any harm; so I went. But now I can see that for the sake of the influence of the thing perhaps a Christian ought not to go. If that is so—and I'm afraid it is—why, I should be willing to give it up. I want to think a little more about it."

Charlie surveyed his friend with a quick, astonished expression; and perhaps there was mingled with the look a new touch of respect. It was something, in his estimation, to be able to give up pleasure for a principle. He did not quite understand the motive that prompted it, but he could appreciate the act.

"H'm!" said he at last. "Well, I can't say I'm ready for just that. It would be pretty tough for me to give up going to the theater for the sake of some old fellow down on Scrogg's Lane, if that's where you locate the 'weak brother.' I'd have to think a long time before I made up my mind to that, I'm afraid."

"You are both talking on the theory that it does no harm to you personally to go, aren't you? Now, I don't admit that, quite," said young Murray. "I can't see why you are not harming yourselves every time you pay out your money to an institution that is such a power in degrading the world and pulling down all moral standards. Why is it not an inevitable harm to yourself to allow yourself to become so fascinated with such a thing that you hesitate about giving it up for the sake of some other one? It seems to me that it cannot fail to lead one farther from Christ. It certainly will not help one in the Christian life. Then, too, the majority of even what you call 'good plays' are poor trash as regards literature, and their code of honor is that of the world, and not of Christ's standards, and they hold up for approval deeds that belong to the world—the world from which we are told to come out and be separate."

Edward was looking very thoughtful; but Charlie was ready to change the subject. It was pointing too near home for his comfort.

"What do you think about dancing? I'm not so fond of it myself, but Ed, there, thinks there's nothing like it. Still, I don't see any harm in it."

"I don't dance," answered young Murray promptly.

"Why not?" asked both men in a breath.

"Well, you certainly know that the only possible reason that can be urged against it is the fact that men and women dance together. You know that the world allows liberties in dancing that it does not consider proper under other circumstances. Why is it that you do not walk up to any young lady you may care to, at an evening gathering, and place your arm about her waist, or hold her hand in yours for an indefinite length of time? You don't consider that the proper thing to do. Why is it right in dancing?"

"Oh, but of course we don't approve of public dances where everybody comes!" Edward hastened to say. "We only dance in the best society, at private houses."

"What difference does that make? Are not the men and women in the best society just as subject to temptation as the people who frequent public balls? Why, it is said that some of the most degraded individuals in the world have come from the highest class of society, and many of them, according to their own confession, have been first led astray through the fascinations of dancing. Not the mere motion, for that is good exercise. You must know yourself that you have often been led to say, or to let your eyes say, much more than you really meant, when you were dancing. The touch of the hand, and the eyes so near to one another—it is so easy to go on, and let the eyes speak. You call it harmless flirting, perhaps, and laugh about it. But you feel a pleasure in it that you would not feel if you were dancing with me, or your sister or your mother. That's my objection to dancing. And then, even if you personally, and the ones in the best society with whom you dance, were exempt from this temptation, there is the 'weak brother' for you to look out for still. He cannot dance in the 'best society,' you know, nor in private houses. He dances with his own society. He says, 'That Christian dances; why shouldn't I?' "

"My, that weak brother again!" exclaimed Charlie carelessly. "I should think he would get to be a terrible nuisance after a while."

"I think perhaps he would," answered the young man, "if it were not for that added phrase, 'For whom Christ died.' If he loved him enough to die for him, I surely ought to be able to give up something for his sake."

"And cards?" asked Edward.

"It seems to me that is much the same. Of course you believe it is wrong to gamble. The games that you play probably do not require that. But there is the possible danger to yourself of the fascination of the game, which may lead you into gambling. And there is the 'weak brother.' He has been led to destruction many and many a time by those bits of pasteboard. You can't tell who about you has an inherited tendency in that direction. The weak brother doesn't always have his name written plainly upon him. He is everywhere. It seems to me that where a thing is known to have danger in it, we had better let it alone. Read Bishop Vincent's little book, *Better Not*, and see if you don't agree with me. If I find a thing that has led many, or any, souls to throw away their chances of eternal life, I think it is a thing for a Christian to keep clear of. It makes pretty solemn business out of life."

The tea-bell broke the silence that followed these words. The afternoon was over. Young Murray felt half sorry that he had said as much as he had done. But he did not know how he could conscientiously have said less.

Charlie Stone was the first to walk out at the door; and as the other two followed him, Edward placed his hand detainingly upon Frank Murray's arm, and said in a low tone, "I thank you for what you have said this afternoon. I have never thought of these things in just that way. I think it will make some difference in my life."

Other Living Books Best-sellers

THE ANGEL OF HIS PRESENCE by Grace Livingston Hill. This book captures the romance of John Wentworth Stanley and a beautiful young woman whose influence causes John to reevaluate his well-laid plans for the future. 07-0047 $2.95.

ANSWERS by Josh McDowell and Don Stewart. In a question-and-answer format, the authors tackle sixty-five of the most-asked questions about the Bible, God, Jesus Christ, miracles, other religions, and creation. 07-0021 $3.95.

THE BEST CHRISTMAS PAGEANT EVER by Barbara Robinson. A delightfully wild and funny story about what happens to a Christmas program when the "Horrible Herdman" brothers and sisters are miscast in the roles of the biblical Christmas story characters. 07-0137 $2.50.

BUILDING YOUR SELF-IMAGE by Josh McDowell. Here are practical answers to help you overcome your fears, anxieties, and lack of self-confidence. Learn how God's higher image of who you are can take root in your heart and mind. 07-1395 $3.95.

THE CHILD WITHIN by Mari Hanes. The author shares insights she gained from God's Word during her own pregnancy. She identifies areas of stress, offers concrete data about the birth process, and points to God's sure promises that he will "gently lead those that are with young." 07-0219 $2.95.

COME BEFORE WINTER AND SHARE MY HOPE by Charles R. Swindoll. A collection of brief vignettes offering hope and the assurance that adversity and despair are temporary setbacks we can overcome! 07-0477 $5.95.

DARE TO DISCIPLINE by James Dobson. A straightforward, plainly written discussion about building and maintaining parent/child relationships based upon love, respect, authority, and ultimate loyalty to God. 07-0522 $3.50.

DAVID AND BATHSHEBA by Roberta Kells Dorr. This novel combines solid biblical and historical research with suspenseful storytelling about men and women locked in the eternal struggle for power, governed by appetites they wrestle to control. 07-0618 $4.95.

FOR MEN ONLY edited by J. Allan Petersen. This book deals with topics of concern to every man: the business world, marriage, fathering, spiritual goals, and problems of living as a Christian in a secular world. 07-0892 $3.95.

FOR WOMEN ONLY by Evelyn and J. Allan Petersen. Balanced, entertaining, diversified treatment of all the aspects of womanhood. 07-0897 $4.95.

400 WAYS TO SAY I LOVE YOU by Alice Chapin. Perhaps the flame of love has almost died in your marriage. Maybe you have a good marriage that just needs a little "spark." Here is a book especially for the woman who wants to rekindle the flame of romance in her marriage; who wants creative, practical, useful ideas to show the man in her life that she cares. 07-0919 $2.95.

Other Living Books Best-sellers

GIVERS, TAKERS, AND OTHER KINDS OF LOVERS by Josh McDowell and Paul Lewis. This book bypasses vague generalities about love and sex and gets right to the basic questions: Whatever happened to sexual freedom? What's true love like? Do men respond differently than women? If you're looking for straight answers about God's plan for love and sexuality, this book was written for you. 07-1031 $2.95.

HINDS' FEET ON HIGH PLACES by Hannah Hurnard. A classic allegory of a journey toward faith that has sold more than a million copies! 07-1429 $3.95.

HOW TO BE HAPPY THOUGH MARRIED by Tim LaHaye. One of America's most successful marriage counselors gives practical, proven advice for marital happiness. 07-1499 $3.50.

JOHN, SON OF THUNDER by Ellen Gunderson Traylor. In this saga of adventure, romance, and discovery, travel with John—the disciple whom Jesus loved—down desert paths, through the courts of the Holy City, to the foot of the cross. Journey with him from his luxury as a privileged son of Israel to the bitter hardship of his exile on Patmos. 07-1903 $4.95.

LIFE IS TREMENDOUS! by Charlie "Tremendous" Jones. Believing that enthusiasm makes the difference, Jones shows how anyone can be happy, involved, relevant, productive, healthy, and secure in the midst of a high-pressure, commercialized society. 07-2184 $2.95.

LOOKING FOR LOVE IN ALL THE WRONG PLACES by Joe White. Using wisdom gained from many talks with young people, White steers teens in the right direction to find love and fulfillment in a personal relationship with God. 07-3825 $3.95.

LORD, COULD YOU HURRY A LITTLE? by Ruth Harms Calkin. These prayer-poems from the heart of a godly woman trace the inner workings of the heart, following the rhythms of the day and the seasons of the year with expectation and love. 07-3816 $2.95.

LORD, I KEEP RUNNING BACK TO YOU by Ruth Harms Calkin. In prayer-poems tinged with wonder, joy, humanness, and questioning, the author speaks for all of us who are groping and learning together what it means to be God's child. 07-3819 $3.50.

MORE THAN A CARPENTER by Josh McDowell. A hard-hitting book for people who are skeptical about Jesus' deity, his resurrection, and his claims on their lives. 07-4552 $2.95.

MOUNTAINS OF SPICES by Hannah Hurnard. Here is an allegory comparing the nine spices mentioned in the Song of Solomon to the nine fruits of the Spirit. A story of the glory of surrender by the author of *HINDS' FEET ON HIGH PLACES.* 07-4611 $3.95.

NOW IS YOUR TIME TO WIN by Dave Dean. In this true-life story, Dean shares how he locked into seven principles that enabled him to bounce back from failure to success. Read about successful men and women—from sports and entertainment celebrities to the ordinary people next door—and discover how you too can bounce back from failure to success! 07-4727 $2.95.

Other Living Books Best-sellers

THE POSITIVE POWER OF JESUS CHRIST by Norman Vincent Peale. All his life the author has been leading men and women to Jesus Christ. In this book he tells of his boyhood encounters with Jesus and of his spiritual growth as he attended seminary and began his world-renowned ministry. 07-4914 $4.50.

REASONS by Josh McDowell and Don Stewart. In a convenient question-and-answer format, the authors address many of the commonly asked questions about the Bible and evolution. 07-5287 $3.95.

ROCK by Bob Larson. A well-researched and penetrating look at today's rock music and rock performers, their lyrics, and their life-styles. 07-5686 $3.50.

THE STORY FROM THE BOOK. The full sweep of *The Book*'s content in abridged, chronological form, giving the reader the "big picture" of the Bible. 07-6677 $4.95.

SUCCESS: THE GLENN BLAND METHOD by Glenn Bland. The author shows how to set goals and make plans that really work. His ingredients of success include spiritual, financial, educational, and recreational balances. 07-6689 $3.50.

TELL ME AGAIN, LORD, I FORGET by Ruth Harms Calkin. You will easily identify with the author in this collection of prayer-poems about the challenges, peaks, and quiet moments of each day. 07-6990 $3.50.

THROUGH GATES OF SPLENDOR by Elisabeth Elliot. This unforgettable story of five men who braved the Auca Indians has become one of the most famous missionary books of all times. 07-7151 $3.95.

WAY BACK IN THE HILLS by James C. Hefley. The story of Hefley's colorful childhood in the Ozarks makes reflective reading for those who like a nostalgic journey into the past. 07-7821 $4.50.

WHAT WIVES WISH THEIR HUSBANDS KNEW ABOUT WOMEN by James Dobson. The best-selling author of *DARE TO DISCIPLINE* and *THE STRONG-WILLED CHILD* brings us this vital book that speaks to the unique emotional needs and aspirations of today's woman. An immensely practical, interesting guide. 07-7896 $3.50.

The books listed are available at your bookstore. If unavailable, send check with order to cover retail price plus $1.00 per book for postage and handling to:

Tyndale DMS
Box 80
Wheaton, Illinois 60189

Prices and availability subject to change without notice. Allow 4–6 weeks for delivery.